THE WORLD'S CLASSICS

THE CASTLES OF ATHLIN AND DUNBAYNE

ANN RADCLIFFE was born in London in 1764. Her father was in trade, but a great part of her youth was passed in the society of wealthy relatives in easy circumstances. At the age of 23 she married William Radcliffe, who later became proprietor and editor of the *English Chronicle*.

Her talents as a novelist were first recognized in 1790 with the publication of *A Sicilian Romance*, which Sir Walter Scott considered to be the first modern English example of the poetical novel. However, her fame rests on her *Romance of the Forest* (1791), *The Mysteries of Udolpho* (1794), and *The Italian* (1797, a romance of the Inquisition).

Mrs Radcliffe's method, which found a number of imitators, was to arouse terror and curiosity by events apparently supernatural. Many of her books were translated into French and Italian.

After 1797 she wrote very little. For the last twelve years of her life she suffered from spasmodic asthma, and succumbed to a sudden attack in 1823.

ALISON MILBANK was John Rylands Research Institute Fellow at the University of Manchester, and now lives and teaches in Cambridge. Her *Daughters of the House: Modes of the Gothic in Victorian Fiction* was published by Macmillan in 1992.

THE WORLD'S CLASSICS

ANN RADCLIFFE

The Castles of Athlin and Dunbayne

Edited with an Introduction by
ALISON MILBANK

Oxford   New York

OXFORD UNIVERSITY PRESS

1995

Oxford University Press, Walton Street, Oxford OX2 6DP

Oxford New York
Athens Auckland Bangkok Bombay
Calcutta Cape Town Dar es Salaam Delhi
Florence Hong Kong Istanbul Karachi
Kuala Lumpur Madras Madrid Melbourne
Mexico City Nairobi Paris Singapore
Taipei Tokyo Toronto
and associated companies in
Berlin Ibadan

Oxford is a trade mark of Oxford University Press

British Library Cataloguing in Publication Data
Data available

Library of Congress Cataloging in Publication Data
Radcliffe, Ann Ward, 1764–1823.
The castles of Athlin and Dunbayne / Ann Radcliffe ; edited with
an introduction by Alison Milbank.
p.   cm. — (The World's classics)
Includes bibliographical references.
1. Scotland—History—1057–1603—Fiction. 2. Man–woman
relationships—Scotland—Highlands—Fiction. 3. Clans—Scotland—
Highlands—Fiction. 4. Highlands (Scotland)—Fiction.
I. Milbank, Alison, 1954– . II. Title. III. Series.
PR5202.C3 1995   823'.6—dc20   94–21123
ISBN 0-19-282357-4

1 3 5 7 9 10 8 6 4 2

Typeset by Graphicraft Typesetters Ltd., Hong Kong
Printed in Great Britain by
BPC Paperbacks Ltd., Aylesbury, Bucks.

CONTENTS

INTRODUCTION

It may come as a surprise to the reader accustomed to the expansive terrors and leisurely descriptions of exotic Mediterranean landscapes of Radcliffe's mature novels to discover that her first attempt at fiction was a short, spare narrative in one volume, set on the bleak north-east coast of Scotland. However, the unusual British setting draws attention to the indigenous cultural context in which Radcliffe's work was conceived and read. A commonplace of criticism of Gothic fiction from the Marquis de Sade onwards has been to view its explosion of popularity in the 1790s and its tropes of malign aristocratic villains, persecuted maidens, and mouldering castles, as directly reactive to the events of the French Revolution, which is held to be such a cataclysm that it renders certain sorts of discourse unsustainable. However, England had already experienced equally disruptive 'signs of history', as Jean-Francois Lyotard terms them, in the Civil War and Glorious Revolution of the seventeenth century, and the Jacobite rebellions of 1715 and 1745. The ferocity with which the Scottish Jacobites were put down after the 1745 rebellion shows, perhaps, that the Hanoverian succession was still a fragile plant. As we shall see, this early Scottish tale of Radcliffe's situates itself in a particularly eighteenth-century mode of writing about the Highlands as a melancholy site, a fallen nation, yet one with privileged access to the past. Scotland's 'fall' after 1745 can be seen as a figure of the original Fall itself, preparing the way, indeed, for a similar reading of the very different fall of the *ancien régime* in the French Revolution.

The plot of Radcliffe's tale unites action of a specifically Scottish medieval nature with the characterization and morality of the eighteenth-century cult of sensibility. The novel traces the revenges taken by Osbert, head of the fallen clan of Athlin, whose chief, Osbert's father, was murdered by Malcolm of Dunbayne some years before. A young Highlander, Alleyn, materially assists the assault on Dunbayne Castle, as well as the rescue of Osbert from imprisonment within its walls. Alleyn loves Osbert's sister Mary, who is torn between the opposing claims of the Countess Matilda and her brother's family pride, and her feelings for Alleyn. A second heroine, Laura, provides a bride for Osbert when he encounters her with her mother, Baroness Malcolm, the chief's sister-in-law, as a fellow prisoner at Dunbayne. Freed by Malcolm's death from duress, the Baroness recognizes in Alleyn the son she had believed dead, thus enclosing all the principal characters in one familial unit. This device is characteristic of the Gothic tale, but it also mimics the Act of Union of 1707 which joined the English and Scottish parliaments.

The title of Radcliffe's novel, *The Castles of Athlin and Dunbayne: A Highland Story* (hereafter referred to as *Athlin and Dunbayne*), would have surprised no one in 1789, since in the preceding two decades an increasingly diverse range of geographical locations had been used in fiction, often employing the same titular form, such as *Rajah and Kisa, An Indian Tale* (1786), and *Orlando and Seraphina, A Turkish Tale* (1787). Horace Walpole's *The Castle of Otranto* of 1765 began the fashion for castles and great houses that continued into the 1780s with Mrs Harley's *St Bernard's Priory* (1786) and Charlotte Smith's *Emmeline: The Orphan of the Castle* (1788). The literary vacuum after the great period of Fielding, Richardson, and Sterne led to a frantic search for novelty of setting—with India and the Americas particularly favoured—and for variety of protagonists, from Jesuits and cossacks to a hackney coach and even a bank-note.[1] The historical tale was well-established, either in the form of an extension to the biography of a historical personage, or of the adventures of a fictional protagonist in the interstices of actual historical events, as in *Longsword, Earl of Salisbury* by Thomas Leland (1762). Incest was an established theme, and there were even novels about the Inquisition. So all the elements that are usually considered Gothic—the ruined castle, malignant tyrant with incestuous desires, the historical setting in an exotic foreign

---

[1] See J. M. S. Tompkins, *The Popular Novel in England 1770–1800* (London, 1932) for many more examples.

locale—were in active use in the eighteenth-century novel before the 1790s; while the last essential figure—the persecuted heroine—is at the heart of novel-writing from Richardson onwards, and would prove equally necessary to the realist fiction of Fanny Burney.

It was Radcliffe who would later reunite these elements into a new synthesis, which would be energized by the focus on the thoughts and motivations of the heroine. But not only does her work develop a distinctive shape out of a huge variety of fictional tropes, it also places itself within certain poetic and dramatic traditions. Even in the eclectic milieu of the novel of the time, her first choice of a Highland setting is a novelty, anticipating Walter Scott by many years, and is also a claim to territory associated then with poetry and poetic drama.[2] A number of verse dramas had been set in Scotland in the eighteenth century, most notably John Home's *Douglas* (1756) and *The Fatal Discovery* (1769). The former, despite the writer's Hanoverian loyalties, attracted political opposition on its first appearance, but was in frequent production until the end of the century. Radcliffe certainly finds her Countess Athlin in *Douglas*'s heroine, also named Matilda, who has lost both a husband in clan warfare and a young son, thus uniting in one character what Radcliffe would separate into two: the Countess Athlin and Baroness Malcolm. Home's Matilda, Lady Randolph, recognizes her lost son in the person of a gallant young Highlander in the manner of Alleyn's restoration in *Athlin and Dunbayne*; but the play ends tragically when he is killed by Lord Randolph as his wife's lover. The villain, Glenalvon, like Radcliffe's Malcolm, feels the hand of God against him, and as in the later novel, the focus moves from his punishment to the sufferings of the Lady Matilda, who commits suicide. This turn from action to feeling shows the drama to be a tragedy of pathos rather than revenge, and it ends on a note of sensibility:

> Nor will I now attempt, with witty folly
> To chase away celestial melancholy.

[2] Montague Summers in *The Gothic Quest* (London, 1937), 48 refers to several other Ossianic novels, but they are all later than *Athlin and Dunbayne*.

The feminine ending of these two lines encapsulates the strange
mixture of neo-classical form with romantic content that char-
acterizes play and novel alike. The influence of poetic drama is
strongly felt in *Athlin and Dunbayne*, both in its tight construc-
tion and its swift succession of scenes of powerful emotion which
one critic, J. M. S. Tompkins, compares to a series of exploding
rockets at a firework display.[3]

The model for the Scottish history play, of course, was Shakespeare's *Macbeth*, a favourite of Radcliffe's, which she later uses
to provide an epigraph to *The Romance of the Forest* (1791),
whose prevailing tone is none the less one of Ardenesque lyricism. *The Winter's Tale* provides much of the plot and the setting
for *A Sicilian Romance* (1790), while the darkness, grotesquery,
and triumphant female virtue of *The Italian* is reminiscent of
Cymbeline. The setting in north-east Scotland of *Athlin and
Dunbayne* is that of Macbeth's stronghold, and the general theme
of usurpation and revenge is the same, but the only detail otherwise borrowed is the name of Malcolm for Radcliffe's tyrannous baron. Perhaps she was thinking of the speech of
Shakespeare's prince which eschews 'the king-becoming graces'
in favour of 'the division of each several crime/Acting it many
ways'. Moreover, there are no witches or even superstitious
highlanders in Radcliffe's novel, although this would be the
element that the dramatization of *Athlin and Dunbayne* by John
Cross would emphasize, by importing a whole cast of fairies and
using a number of supernatural effects.[4] The reason for the
excision of any reference to the supernatural in a work which
places itself in Macbethian territory may lie in some remarks of
Samuel Johnson in his edition of Shakespeare's plays, which was
then popular and highly authoritative:

A poet who should now make the whole action of his tragedy depend
upon enchantment and produce the chief events by the assitance of
supernatural agents, would be censured as transgressing the bounds

---

[3] Tompkins, *The Popular Novel*, 58.
[4] John Cross, *Hallowe'en; or The Castles of Athlin and Dunbayne, 'A New
Grand Scotch Spectacle'* (London, 1809).

of probability, be banished from the theatre to the nursery, and condemned to write fairytales instead of tragedies.

(*Works of Shakespeare*, iv. 393.)

However, Johnson goes on to show that it was poetically appropriate for Shakespeare to include witches in *Macbeth* because
belief in them was current in his time. The post-Enlightenment
Radcliffe in *Athlin and Dunbayne* could not, although her
governess in *A Sicilian Romance* argues strongly that the existence of supernatural beings is part of the Divine economy. A
posthumously-published work, *Gaston de Blondeville*, set in the
Middle Ages, uses a ghost as an agent of retribution. But that
work is presented as a discovered authentic medieval fragment.
In her other novels Radcliffe creates characters who are both of
their period, and also the products of an eighteenth-century
author. This leads to some uncanny and troubling effects such
as the notorious black veil in *The Mysteries of Udolpho*, which, it
is finally revealed, hides nothing supernatural but merely a wax
effigy. Radcliffe's readers, like Alleyn feeling the dead hand in
the vaults of Dunbayne, are always being brought into collision
with materiality made uncanny, and modern modes of knowledge are themselves made strange as the supernatural is revealed
as the natural. The unease and sense of disappointment that
ensues is, in part, the message.

Despite its disavowal of supernatural effects, *Athlin and
Dunbayne* was chastized in the September 1789 *Critical Review*:

To those who are delighted with *the marvellous*, whom wonders, and
wonders only, can charm, the present production will afford a considerable degree of amusement. This kind of entertainment, however, can
be little relished but by the young and unformed mind. To men who
have passed or even attained the meridian of life, a series of events,
which seem not to have their foundation in nature, will ever be insipid,
if not disgustful.

Although the notice goes on to compare the work to that of 'Mr
Bayes', a misprint for Bage, then highly regarded for his exciting
novels of ideas, this stately reviewer obviously considers *Athlin
and Dunbayne* a fairytale. And yet, the choice of the Scotland of
the Middle Ages as setting did indeed render much of the action

'natural'. Radcliffe's novel shows that she had read the travel literature on the Highlands of the time. In this context Johnson provides an authorization rather than a check:

These [Scottish] castles afford another evidence that the fictions of romantick chivalry had for their basis the real manners of the feudal times, when every lord of a seignory lived in his hold lawless and unaccountable with all the licentiousness and insolence of uncontested superiority and unprincipled power.

(*A Journey to the Western Islands of Scotland* (1775), 120.)

In this and similar passages in the same work Johnson offers the anthropology that justifies the plot of Radcliffe's novel and the atrocities of Malcolm.

It may seem bizarre that I should argue that the embryo Gothic novelist operates in response to Johnsonian principles, but this is the same Johnson who, while in Scotland, fell to his knees in prayer on the island of Iona, and hung on the words of the Jacobite heroine, Flora MacDonald. Johnson sought something different from his own culture on the journey through Scotland, and, with the edition of Shakespeare in which he seeks to defend the dramatist from neo-classical strictures, *A Journey to the Western Islands of Scotland* is one of his least Augustan productions. Indeed, Johnson's preface to *Lear* provides all the principles on which Radcliffe's narrative technique will come to rely:

There is perhaps no play which keeps the attention so strongly fixed; which so agitates our passions and interests our curiosity. The artful involutions of distinct interests, the striking opposition of contrary characters, and sudden changes of fortune, and the quick succession of events, fill the mind with a perpetual tumult of indignation, pity, and hope. There is not a scene which does not contribute to the aggravation of distress or conduct of the action, and scarce a line which does not conduce to the progress of the scene. So powerful is the current of the poet's imagination that the mind, which once ventures within it, is hurried irresistibly along.   (iv. 488.)

Athlin and Dunbayne already achieves the chiaroscuro, pace, economy, and 'aggravation' of this list, although the pity and imagination would not have full play until Radcliffe's later fiction. The Johnsonian criteria could, in fact, apply to a range of eighteenth-century tragedy, and it is to this tradition that Radcliffe owes her technique, even if she takes plot motifs from novelists like Clara Reeve and Sophia Lee.

Johnson refers constantly to Shakespeare as a poet, and it is in the latter's lyricism and the poems and songs interspersed throughout the plays that Radcliffe finds another element of her individual style, that is, her use of her own poetry to punctuate the narrative. She was not the first novelist so to embellish her work, for Charlotte Smith, who was first known as a poet, allowed her heroes and heroines to declaim. However, Smith's verses interrupt the narrative artificially, and rarely have a dramatic function. There are just three poems in *Athlin and Dunbayne* but they are the heralds of many more to come. Each, moreover, as in Shakespeare, signals a period of rest in the relentless onrush of the narrative, especially Osbert's 'Sonnet' (pp. 39–40), which establishes a moment of 'still sound' in the landscape, as evening drifts through the woods, while Laura's song to the lute, heard first as pure music, literally arrests Osbert in his course of self-destruction. Moreover, there is a dramatic function to each: Laura's music saves Osbert's life while telling her own story, and Osbert's sonnet is thrown down to be picked up by the ladies and used to establish social relations with them.

The figurative language of the two songs is that of fancy, a favourite poetic theme from the sixteenth century onwards, and one that is directly associated with Shakespeare in the eighteenth. Milton's 'Shakespeare, fancy's sweetest child!' is Johnson's first example in the entry for fancy in his 1755 dictionary. In Laura's poem (an imitation of James Beattie's 'The Triumph of Melancholy') youthful fancy or imagination fails, as sad experience blights her life: 'Pale Grief Hope's trembling rays dispers'd/ And Fancy's dreams dissolv'd' (p. 34). But in Osbert's reply fancy enables an inward vision that imprisonment cannot prevent and produces a sound, the creation of 'the fairy hour'. Radcliffe's later fiction includes several more odes to fancy, as well as fairy poems, and even an ode to Titania, Shakespeare's Queen of the Fairies. Every one of these poems performs an act of imaginative expansion, giving expression to fancy as the

embodiment of a kind of 'natural magic', in which the supernatural is elided with nature. Again, one can find Johnsonian
support for this, as he regards such an accommodation as a
peculiarly Shakespearian achievement: 'Shakespeare approximates
the remote and familiarizes the wonderful'.[5] The most celebrated
practitioner of this art is the poet William Collins, who was a
Shakespearian devotee, and who imitated the song from *Cymbeline*
with uncanny effect. Collins continues another aspect of Shakespearian lyricism in his attention to a particular way of writing
about the evening. His 'Ode to Evening' was very influential,
and was imitated several times by Radcliffe. The fairy hour of
twilight, when Titania seeks her bank 'whereon the wild thyme
blows', is the privileged time of day in eighteenth-century verse,
most famously in the opening line of Thomas Gray's 'Elegy in
a Country Churchyard': 'The curfew tolls the knell of parting
day', which was itself indebted to Dante's *Purgatorio*, Canto 8.
The magic of twilight is the particular mood of hushed suspension it engenders, in a moment that is neither night nor day, and
in which, in Collins's Ode, the personified figure of Eve is felt as
an indwelling presence within the landscape. Radcliffe uses this
effect in Osbert's sonnet in which 'ev'ning wand'ring through
her woodlands dear' is dissolved into sound like the nymph
Echo, and similarly reverberates: 'the woods and wilds the
feeble notes prolong'. Language is here itself dissolving in the
half-light, in the lost 'e's of 'ev'ning' and 'wand'ring', leaving
just a 'v' of pure vibration. The total effect is of a reposeful
indeterminacy, a balance of powers, and a pastoral respite from
the strong challenge of the sublime Highland landscape of mountains and cataracts.

These two short poems are emphasized because they provide
a key to reading the novel as a whole. *Athlin and Dunbayne* may
begin fierily in oaths of revenge, in which the young earl dis-
dains the softer female virtues for a plan to attack his father's
murderer and obtain vengeance. Soon, however, he is captured
and remains a passive prisoner for much of the novel. His res-
cuer, the virtuous Alleyn, similarly spends an inordinately long

[5] Samuel Johnson, *Prefaces to Shakespeare's Plays* (Menston, 1969), xi.

time suspended from the action within the castle vaults—an arrest less beneficent than the free suspension of twilight. One clue to the reason for the abrupt turn to passivity lies in Osbert's predilection for poetry, which leads him 'to wander among the romantic scenes of the Highlands, where the wild variety of nature inspired him with all the enthusiasm of his favourite art' (p. 5). Particularly, we are told, 'he delighted in the terrible and the grand, more than in the softer landscape; and wrapt in the bright visions of fancy, would often lose himself in awful solitudes'. Just as fancy allows one to lose oneself in the twilight indeterminacy, so it leads one to seek out the lofty and terrible in art or nature, which the eighteenth century sums up in the word 'sublime'. The sublime strikes reverence in the observer, and, especially in the theory put forward by Edmund Burke, confirms the individual as a subject, that is, both a human being, a creature, and a comparatively powerless one. The poetic influence on the young earl is, anachronistically, James Beattie's long Spenserian poem *The Minstrel; or, the Progress of Genius* (1777), which describes a young Scottish shepherd bard:

> And oft the craggy cliff he loved to climb,
> When all in mist the world below was lost.
> What dreadful pleasure! there to stand sublime,
> Like shipwrecked mariner on desert coast.   (I, xxi)

Like Osbert, overcome by the solitudes of the highland wilderness, the shepherd bard Edwin's high position of dominance yet brings with it isolation and a sense of weakness in the figure of the shipwrecked sailor. It is, as Burke observed, a taking of pleasure in what is unpleasurable.

So the delicate yielding to nature in the twilight moment and the sublime delight in one's ow_ subjection of the sublime can both place the subject in a position of arrest. To these aesthetic elements Radcliffe has a third to add, which indeed is inextricably linked to evening poetry, that is, melancholy. This mood of pensive sorrow is a favourite of poets from Collins to Akenside, Blair to Thomson, and has a particular Scottish association in the work of James Macpherson, which purported to be the productions of an ancient Celtic prince, Ossian. The Ossian poems cleverly re-created the material uncanny of seventeenth-century Bible translation, with wild and romantic landscape description and heroes and heroines of sensibility. Radcliffe quotes from the work in Chapter 2 of *The Romance of the Forest*. Although the warriors of Ossian are frequently involved in violent action, the tone is elegiac, and Johnson's Scottish journal states that 'the Highlands of Scotland could scarcely have offered Ossian more images of simple greatness or more circumstances for melancholy inspiration' (392–3). Of the proponents of melancholy in eighteenth-century poetry a large number were Scottish, including James Thomson, Robert Blair, James Beattie, and Macpherson himself. Its independence lost after the Act of Union of 1702, its clan organization destroyed after the 1745 rebellion, its population greatly dispersed by forced clearances, eighteenth-century Scotland was a fallen nation, now grieving its own demise. So, despite the medieval setting, the Highlands is a highly suitable location for *The Castles of Athlin and Dunbayne*, in which every virtuous character—Lady Athlin, Mary, Baroness Malcolm, Laura, Osbert, and finally, Alleyn—falls prey to grief and melancholy. This state is presented in the novel as the natural response to loss, and, like the poetic evening which is the appropriate time for the expression of melancholy, it causes passivity and a suspension of activity. In eighteenth-century verse it has a philosophic dimension, giving expression to the sorrow inherent in existence itself, 'this fleeting state of things, the vain delights', as Thomas Warton puts it in 'The Pleasures of Melancholy'. It is Contemplation that conducts the philosopher to Melancholy's 'ruin'd seat's' and 'twilight cells and bow'rs' where he can meditate upon death and transience. In Thomson's *Seasons* melancholy forms an ideal character: 'The glowing cheek, the mild dejected Air/The soften'd Feature, and the beating Heart/Pierced deep with many a virtuous pang' ('Winter', 1006–8). This description could apply to any of Radcliffe's pensive heroines in their various plights.

There are two reasons why *Athlin and Dunbayne*, and the later novels, privilege melancholy. First, as Paul Sherwin has argued in relation to William Collins, melancholy is conceived as the appropriate response of the thoughtful person to human

estrangement from the natural world.[6] This is registered in the
very act of making the landscape a subject for writing, and thus
witnessing to the separation from that which one describes.
Using the terminology of Freud's essay, 'Mourning and Melancholia', Sherwin argues that nature poetry 'becomes intrinsically
elegiac, a poetry of nostalgic longing, in which celebration (of a
lost object) and lamentation (for the mourning subject) are in-
distinguishable'.[7] Radcliffe's work registers this nostalgia both in
the melancholy tone of its verse and prose evocations of the
landscape, and also in its employment of the trope of incarcera-
tion inside a castle cut off from the world of nature. Radcliffe's
heroines often take a picaresque trajectory as they move through
a succession of different natural scenes which are celebrated in
contrast to the 'unnatural' behaviour of their human inhabitants.
Secondly, melancholy is important in Radcliffe because it offers
its own healing—it is a *pharmakon* in the Greek sense of a poison
that can make one better. And this healing, as we shall see, is not
a restoration of a nostalgic return to the womb and undifferen-
tiation, but a more bracing acceptance of one's 'fallen' state. It
was understood by Collins that the pensive evening could provide consolation, and bring out positive virtues—'Fancy, Friendship, Science, rose-lipped Health'—while Thomson wrote that
melancholy marked the beginning of renewed social relations
through 'the sigh for suffering Worth/Lost in Obscurity; the
noble Scorn/Of tyrant Pride' which would engender 'all the
social offspring of the Heart' ('Winter', 1023–4). This double
move of Thomson's is made in *Athlin and Dunbayne* in the
sympathy for the obscurely born Alleyn and the scorning of the
tyrannous Malcolm. The revelation of Alleyn's noble anteced-
ents is not a complete failure of radical nerve on Radcliffe's part,
because Osbert's reluctance to allow the benevolent peasant to
marry his sister is overtly criticized by the narrator as the result
of 'the darkness of prejudice and ancient pride' (p. 109).

The key to the ethics of Thomson's poem and Radcliffe's

[6] Paul Sherwin, *Precious Bane: William Collins and the Miltonic Legacy* (Aus-
tin, 1977), 110.
[7] Sherwin, *Precious Bane*, 103.

novels (as the later fiction makes clearly articulate) lies in a union of melancholy with the sublime. Although a number of poets wrote on both themes, the link is not often made. An important site for melancholic reflection is the ruin, because of its allegorical message of the wreckage time can cause; and the sublime too can be evoked by the huge or lowering ruin, and particularly by the ruined nature of the earth itself. Thomson and Radcliffe are both adherents of the theories of the seventeenth-century Bishop Burnet, which were popularized in Shaftesbury, of the effect on the natural world of the Fall of Man and his expulsion from the Garden of Eden. The changing seasons are seen as the result of this cataclysm, while the mountains with their dangers and sheer falls are the result of the great Flood sent by God to judge the world, and not part of the original creation. Hence they too are cultural, as indeed is all nature, which is as much a ruin as an ivied abbey or mouldering arch. To respond to the sublime in nature is thus to acknowledge God's power to judge and even destroy the created order.

Melancholic and sublime responses to nature are therefore marks of an awareness that there is no possible return to union with 'Mother Nature' and that we are ruined subjects in a ruined world, selves, as Julia Kristeva's work on melancholy describes it, primitively wounded and incomplete.[8] The healing which melancholy can provide of its own ruin is found in the moment of twilight, which is not so much a nostalgic return that cancels the Fall and difference, as an achieved balance whose magic consists in the awareness that separation exists, and mediation is necessary. So Thomson's 'sober *Evening*/Takes her wonted station in the Middle Air', with the emphasis on 'middle', and literally 'even's out' differences between air and land, and separate objects, by means of the dusky veil of evening obscurity. The witness to the Fall is very clear when one recognizes the common buried source in eighteenth-century twilight poems in Milton. 'Il Penseroso' was vastly popular in the first half of the century, and set a fashion for the pensive twilight; but so also was *Paradise Lost*, which also has some powerful

---

[8] Julia Kristeva, *Le Soleil Noir: Dépression et mélancolie* (Paris, 1987), 22.

evening scenes, most notably that in Book iv which describes Adam and Eve resting from their gardening to enjoy the fragrance of the evening in the embraces of a perfect pre-lapsarian erotic reciprocity. In the golden hair of Eve falling over Adam's breast is expressed a balance between sexual difference and the 'one flesh' of marriage. Milton's Eve wandering through the flowery glades of Paradise is, I would argue, a presence in many twilight poems of this period, providing an image of humanity and the natural world in unblemished harmony. It is, however, a melancholy act of remembrance not only because of the Fall which Eve would undergo by listening to the serpent and eating of the tree of knowledge, but because that blissful scene in Milton's fourth book is the beginning of the process, and the eye that views Eve is that of the already-fallen Satan, who is made 'still in gaze' at the sight.

So the reunion of subject and landscape in the evening poems in Radcliffe and elsewhere is redemptive precisely in its recognition of a shared sense of loss in both human and natural worlds. It also points to the possibility of regenerated relations between the sexes. Feminist readings of *Paradise Lost* were common in some eighteenth-century circles, which stressed, despite Milton's sexual hierarchy, the dignity and importance of Eve, and the companionate nature of her marriage with Adam. Radcliffe's fiction similarly seeks to establish unions of equality through a shared melancholy, and her couples retire to Rousseauian pastoral retreats to create new Edens rather than take their place in the great world. In these pastoral *La Vallées*, virtue and love of nature may go hand-in-hand, in the manner of Shaftesbury's optimistic philosophy in which virtue is a natural faculty, and perfect virtue is perfected taste in morals. As 'taste' involves a response to God in nature this phrase takes on a deeper resonance than might at first appear. It is Shaftesbury, too, who lies behind *Athlin and Dunbayne*'s sense of poetic justice. Baron Malcolm is eventually killed accidentally by Osbert in ignorance of his true identity, and the fatal wounding is presented as almost self-inflicted. This accommodates Shaftesbury's claim that anyone who fails to serve the general good 'is on that account his own enemy, nor can he any

otherwise be good or useful to himself', *Characteristics of Men,
Manners, Opinions, Times, etc.* (1711), I. 388.

The final characteristic feature of Radcliffe's later work seen
for the first time in *Athlin and Dunbayne* is the castle itself,
which, as been commonly observed, is a protagonist rather than
a background. Like Robert Adam's designs for such Scottish
castles as Culzean, Radcliffe's castles have movement, being
articulations of light and shade, convexity and concavity, and
outside and inside, in a manner hitherto confined to architecture. A novel like Reeve's *The Old English Baron* enjoys a plethora
of castles, but they have little dramatic function outside the
haunting scene, being more like the careful Gothic reconstruc-
tions of contemporary stage design. Reeve offered an allegorical
model for the castle in her *Progress of Romance* (1785), in which
romances are divided, like the house on sand or on rock of
Christ's parable, into castles with or without secure foundations.
Ostensibly *Athlin and Dunbayne*'s two castles seems to reverse
this figure. Athlin 'venerable from its antiquity, and from its
Gothic structure, but more venerable from the virtues it enclosed' (p. 3) is the 'good' castle; but its open, candid declaration
of its age and thus its subjection to the inroads of time makes it
seem less impregnable than Dunbayne. Its site as nursery of the
virtues is reminiscent of Madame Genlis' *Tales of the Castle*
(translated 1785), in which a noble French family retreat from
the dissipations of Paris to inhabit an ancient castle and learn
virtue and social responsibility in stories round the hearth.
Dunbayne, as befits the tyrant's stronghold, is a complete set of
mysteries, and contains two hidden women prisoners, secret
panels and passages, extensive underground vaults, and tunnels
leading out to end in caves. The narrative stresses both the
exterior impenetrability of the edifice, which is 'built with Gothic
magnificence upon a high and dangerous rock' with towers that
'still frowned in proud sublimity' (p. 13), and its porous interior
of labyrinthine interconnections. Indeed, it is its strenuous claim
to superhuman authority and impregnability that creates the
need for so many dungeons and secret ways which then become
the means of its undoing. In terms of the value-system established
by the novel Dunbayne's double unknowability of impenetrable

outside and mazelike inside expresses the hubris of the tower of Babel in Genesis, where claims to sublimity were met with destruction and the creation of different and mutually incomprehensible languages. Dunbayne's sublimity similarly seeks to dominate the natural world and separate itself from it. It is not accidental that, although Athlin too is built upon a rock, its base is in the sea, and spray is thrown up against its windows. The earl deliberately goes out onto the terrace to observe a furious storm and is thereby instrumental in rescuing the victims of a shipwreck. Athlin Castle and its social organization is one that reaches out to the created order and lives in awareness of its subjection to natural processes. In this way, following Thomson, it is enabled to serve the needs of others. A taste for the sublime outside the self (whereas Dunbayne claims that quality for itself) leads directly to ethical action. In the same way Osbert's poetic wanderings in wild country effect the encounter with Alleyn that will bring about his revenge of his father's murder, together with the ethical, social, and romantic resolution of the novel. Dunbayne's physical separation, on the other hand, is accompanied by social isolation and a failure by the baron to act benevolently towards his people 'who sinking under severe exactions, suffer to lie uncultivated, tracts which would otherwise yield riches to their lord' (p. 7). At Athlin it is a part of the castle, not the land, that is allowed to lie unused and ruined, and this is another sign of the earl's willingness to elide the cultural to the natural, as the ruin is 'naturalized' in the manner in which the sea acts upon the walls of the building.

There is a programmatic quality to the novel's structure which offers two chiefs, two castles, two mourning noblewomen, two pensive heroines, two sons restored, and so on. The doubling applies also to the characters' psychology, as each is routinely torn by two contending emotions. The effect is that of a diptych in which each set of characters and positions mirrors the other, and comments upon it. The sense of an impossible deadlock, of there being no way forward in the plot, is a direct result of this structure. Only Alleyn is different. His position in clan terms is obscure, since he belongs to the Fitzhenrys, who are a separate tribe with some relation to the Athlins, lying inoperative under

Dunbayne's tyranny. He appears as if from nowhere out of an 'Elysian Vale', and holds his identity purely in terms of natural virtue, since his tie to the late Athlin is reverence for his moral worth rather than simple feudal loyalty. A peasant, but without a status in the social pattern, Alleyn functions as a 'wild card' who alone can initiate action or mediate between the opposing groups. Having himself escaped with great difficulty from Dunbayne, Alleyn returns to effect the rescue of Osbert who seems to represent the aesthetic grounds upon which virtue is based. Only when Alleyn's true worth is recognized by Osbert can narrative resolution be achieved. In the later fiction Radcliffe will unite the aesthetic and the moral in the one figure of the heroine, who as victim of tyranny can reprove her persecutor, and as enthusiast for nature make the act of submission to the sublime that will release Divine poetic justice. In the dream-like melancholic quietism of *Athlin and Dunbayne* the schematic setting allows only a tentative naming of roles.

Alleyn and Osbert mirror each other in their period of despair during imprisonment, akin to the mystic's 'dark night of the soul'. Osbert, as befits the poet, suffers predominantly mental tortures which cause him to contemplate self-destruction; while Alleyn's sufferings are physical. He is kept in a dungeon, whereas Osbert has a window in his room in the tower. The threat to Osbert's sense of identity is reflected in Alleyn's actual experience of indeterminacy as he enters the subterranean darkness of the castle vaults. There space unexpectedly contracts and expands, separations seem to collapse, and release only occurs at the moment of what appears to be final defeat. Osbert, similarly, endures this gloomy suspension and miraculous escape passively achieved. The function of these peregrinations in the hushed stillness of the subterranean castle seems to be to present a negative melancholia and a sublime that is truly 'subliminal' in its threat to the self. This is the appropriate trial for those who would seek the true sublime and confirm their sense of personhood in an aesthetic and moral reunion with nature, human and non-human.

The various attempts at escape from Dunbayne are constantly blocked, as is the fate of almost every positive act in the novel.

Instead, a number of recognition scenes, usually unsought, move the action on. So Alleyn twice approaches someone in distress, to find himself the saviour of an abducted Mary. Twice his love for Mary is revealed in epiphanic moments with a miniature on a bracelet and a portrait respectively. The Baron, and later the Count de Saintmorin, are revealed under disguises at the moment of judgement. Such events culminate in the recognition by the Baroness Malcolm that Alleyn is her lost son. These moments of blinding light in a dark narrative are again part of the aesthetic argument which is resolved in the third poem in the text entitled, 'Morning', written by Osbert, although it is sung by his sister. It begins thus:

> DARKNESS! through thy chilling glooms,
>   Weakly trembles twilight gray;
> Twilight fades—and morning comes,
>   And melts thy shadows swift away! (p. 93)

In this poem the blessed compensatory moment of evening is now superseded as dawn brings 'spirit—light—and life anew', with a gale in the air that 'wanders wild/O'er mountain top and woodland glade', unlike the almost motionless 'still sound' of evening in Osbert's earlier sonnet. The still unresolved question of Alleyn's suit causes the singer to strike her lute wildly after her own plangent coda, but the song heralds a new dawn also for her and Alleyn, when her second abduction, and his assumption of Dunbayne, are followed by their marriage. The language of chiaroscuro of the morning song is conventional; but in relation to the graveyard poetic tradition to which Radcliffe has been shown to be attentive it is full of religious content. For example, Beattie's minstrel questions the justice of the world's treatment of virtue, then gives his own reply thus: 'Heaven's immortal spring shall yet arrive/And man's majestic beauty bloom again/ Bright through th'eternal year of Love's triumphant reign'. The eternal Spring of the golden age is given an apocalyptic meaning here as the time of the last judgement and the inrush of God's light into the world. Thomson shares this figure of an eternal Spring, conceived primarily as a morning, the 'Day of the Lord'.

In the ending of *Athlin and Dunbayne* the darkness and melancholy lifts, and a metaphysical dawn is heralded:

Virtue may for a time be pursued by misfortune,—and justice be obscured by the transient triumphs of vice;—but the Power whose peculiar attributes they are, clears away the clouds of error, and even in this world establishes his THRONE OF JUSTICE.   (p. 113)

By aligning themselves aesthetically with the sublime power of God in nature, and politically with the rejection of tyranny, Radcliffe's protagonists have enabled the operation of poetic justice, and the apocalyptic inroad of judgement as 'justice bares the arm of God' and causes Him to act. The ending presages the Day of the Lord, when the ruin will be restored, as Isaiah declares, and there shall be no more weeping. Melancholy then will no longer be an appropriate response.

With this mixture of melancholy and apocalypticism, *Athlin and Dunbayne* was a strange work to emerge from the fashionable circulating library of Hookham in 1789. It is oddly old-fashioned in looking backward to the early part of the century to orchestrate a number of themes from the elegiac poetic tradition. Yet it also looks forward to Romanticism in its opposition of Fancy's balanced lyricism to the jagged threat of the sublime, although it invokes Biblical eschatology to resolve this tension. Wordsworth and Coleridge would find their particular means of resolving the dichotomy in the imaginative power of the human mind itself. In the mean time, Radcliffe lays the foundation, in her first novel, of an ethical technique and a poetics of living in the darkness of a fissured world, while continuing to hope, like Thomson, that

> The storms of WINTRY TIME will quickly pass
> And one unbounded SPRING encircle all.   ('Winter', 1068)

NOTE ON THE TEXT

The edition used here is the second Dublin edition of 1794. *The Castles of Athlin and Dunbayne: A Highland Story* was published anonymously in 1789 by Thomas Hookham, a fashionable circulating library proprietor and publisher in New Bond Street, London. A second edition appeared after the success of *The Romance of the Forest*, in 1793, and a third in 1799. The novel was translated into French in 1819, was twice dramatized, and was often reissued during the nineteenth century. There are hardly any alterations from the first edition, unlike other Radcliffe novels, although the long 's' was dropped in the nineteenth century. Original spelling and punctuation have here been retained, with some minor alterations, most notably that double quotation marks have been replaced by single.

SELECT BIBLIOGRAPHY

J. and A. AIKIN, *Miscellaneous Pieces in Prose* (London, 1773).

ARCHIBALD ALISON, *Essays on the Nature and Principles of Taste* (Dublin, 1790).

PIERRE ARNAUD, *Ann Radcliffe et le fantastique: Essai de psychobiographie* (Paris, 1976).

GILLIAN BEER, '"Our unnatural no-voice:" The Heroic Epistle, Pope, and Women's Gothic', *Yearbook of English Studies*, 12 (1982), 125–51.

PATRICK BRYDONE, *A Tour Thro' Sicily and Malta. In a Series of Letters to William Beckford* (London, 1775).

EDMUND BURKE, *A Philosophical Enquiry into the Origin of our Ideas of the Sublime and Beautiful*, ed. Adam Phillips, World's Classics (Oxford, 1990).

MARGARET ANNE DOODY, 'Deserts, Ruins, and Troubled Waters: Female Dreams in Fiction and the Development of the Gothic Novel', *Genre*, 10 (1977), 529–72.

DAVID S. DURANT, *Ann Radcliffe's Novels: Experiments in Setting* (New York, 1980).

WILLIAM GILPIN, *Observations on the Highlands of Scotland* (London, 1789).

NORMAN HOLLAND and LEONORA SHERMAN, 'Gothic Possibilities', *New Literary History*, 8/2 (Winter 1977), 279–94.

SAMUEL JOHNSON, *Prefaces to Shakespeare's Plays* (Menston, 1969).

—— *A Journey to the Western Islands of Scotland* (London, 1775).

CLARA MCINTYRE, *Ann Radcliffe in Relation to Her Time* (Yale, 1920).

ELLEN MOERS, *Literary Women* (London, 1977).

SAMUEL H. MONK, *The Sublime: A Study of Critical Theories in Eighteenth-Century England* (Ann Arbor, 1960).

THOMAS PENNANT, *A Tour in Scotland 1769* (London, 1772).

DAVID PUNTER, *The Literature of Terror: A History of Gothic Fiction from 1765 to the Present Day* (London, 1980).

EINO RAILO, *The Haunted Castle: A Study of the Elements of English Romanticism* (London and New York, 1927).

AMY REED, *The Background of Gray's 'Elegy': A Study in the Taste for Melancholy Poetry 1700–1751* (New York, 1924).

SIR WALTER SCOTT, 'Mrs Ann Radcliffe', in *The Lives of the Novelists* (Edinburgh, 1825).

MONTAGUE SUMMERS, *The Gothic Quest* (London, 1937).

J. M. S. TOMPKINS, *The Popular Novel in England 1770–1800* (London, 1932).

MALCOLM WARE, *Sublimity in the Novels of Ann Radcliffe* (Uppsala and Copenhagen, 1963).

A. A. S. WIETEN, *Mrs Radcliffe: Her Relation towards Romanticism* (Amsterdam, 1926).

A CHRONOLOGY OF ANN RADCLIFFE

1764 (9 July) Born in London, daughter of William and Ann Ward (née Oates).

1787 Married William Radcliffe.

1789 *The Castles of Athlin and Dunbayne: A Highland Story*. Published anonymously.

1790 *A Sicilian Romance* (2 vols.). Published anonymously.

1791 *The Romance of the Forest, Interspersed with Some Pieces of Poetry* (3 vols.). Published anonymously, but acknowledged as the work of Radcliffe in the second edition (1792).

1794 *The Mysteries of Udolpho: A Romance, Interspersed with Some Pieces of Poetry* (4 vols.).

1795 *A Journey Made in the Summer of 1794, through Holland and the Western Frontier of Germany, with a Return down the Rhine, to which Are Added Observations during a Tour to the Lakes of Lancashire, Westmoreland and Cumberland.*

1797 *The Italian; or, The Confessional of the Black Penitents: A Romance* (3 vols.).

1815 *The Poems of Mrs. Ann Radcliffe* (an unauthorized reprint of the poems in the novels).

1823 (7 February) Died.

1826 'Of the Supernatural in Poetry', *New Monthly Magazine and Literary Journal*, 16, 145–52.
     Gaston de Blondeville; or, The Court of Henry III, Keeping Festival in Ardenne: A Romance and *St. Alban's Abbey: A Metrical Tale* (published together in 4 vols.).

THE CASTLES OF
ATHLIN AND DUNBAYNE
A Highland Story

—for justice bares the arm of God,
and the grasp'd vengeance only waits his nod.*

CAWTHORN

CHAPTER I

ON the north-east coast of Scotland, in the most romantic* part of the Highlands, stood the Castle of Athlin; an edifice built on the summit of a rock whose base was in the sea.* This pile was venerable from its antiquity, and from its Gothic structure; but more venerable from the virtues which it enclosed. It was the residence of the still beautiful widow, and the children of the noble Earl of Athlin,* who was slain by the hand of Malcolm, a neighbouring chief, proud, oppressive, revengeful; and still residing in all the pomp of feudal greatness,* within a few miles of the castle of Athlin. Encroachment on the domain of Athlin, was the occasion of the animosity which subsisted between the chiefs. Frequent broils had happened between their clans,* in which that of Athlin had generally been victorious. Malcolm, whose pride was touched by the defeat of his people; whose ambition was curbed by the authority, and whose greatness was rivalled by the power of the Earl, conceived for him that deadly hatred which opposition to its favourite passions naturally excites in a mind like his, haughty and unaccustomed to controul; and he meditated his destruction. He planned his purpose with all that address which so eminently marked his character, and in a battle which was attended by the chiefs* of each party in person, he contrived, by a curious finesse,* to entrap the Earl, accompanied by a small detachment, in his wiles, and there slew him.* A general rout of his clan ensued, which was followed by a dreadful slaughter; and a few only escaped to tell the horrid catastrophe to Matilda. Overwhelmed by the news, and deprived of those numbers which would make revenge successful, Matilda forbore to sacrifice the lives of her few remaining people to a feeble attempt at retaliation, and she was constrained to endure in silence her sorrows and her injuries.

Inconsolable for his death, Matilda had withdrawn from the public eye, into this ancient seat of feudal government, and there, in the bosom of her people and her family, had devoted herself to the education of her children. One son and one daughter were all that survived to her care, and their growing virtues promised to repay all her tenderness. Osbert was in his nineteenth year: nature had given him a mind ardent and susceptible, to which education had added refinement and expansion. The visions of genius* were bright in his imagination, and his heart, unchilled by the touch of disappointment, glowed with all the warmth of benevolence.*

When first we enter on the theatre of the world, and begin to notice its features, young imagination heightens every scene, and the warm heart expands to all around it. The happy benevolence of our feelings prompts us to believe that every body is good, and excites our wonder why every body is not happy. We are fired with indignation at the recital of an act of injustice, and at the unfeeling vices of which we are told. At a tale of distress our tears flow a full tribute to pity: at a deed of virtue our heart unfolds, our soul aspires, we bless the action, and feel ourselves the doer. As we advance in life, imagination is compelled to relinquish a part of her sweet delirium; we are led reluctantly to truth through the paths of experience; and the objects of our fond attention are viewed with a severer eye. Here an altered scene appears;—frowns where late were smiles; deep shades where late was sunshine: mean passions, or disgusting apathy stain the features of the principal figures. We turn indignant from a prospect so miserable, and court again the sweet illusions of our early days; but ah! they are fled for ever! Constrained, therefore, to behold objects in their more genuine hues, their deformity is by degrees less painful to us. The fine touch of moral susceptibility, by frequent irritation becomes callous; and too frequently we mingle with the world, till we are added to the number of its votaries.

Mary, who was just seventeen, had the accomplishments of riper years, with the touching simplicity of youth. The graces of her person were inferior only to those of her mind, which illumined her countenance with inimitable expression.

Twelve years had now elapsed since the death of the Earl, and time had blunted the keen edge of sorrow. Matilda's grief had declined into a gentle, and not unpleasing melancholy, which gave a soft and interesting shade to the natural dignity of her character. Hitherto her attention had been solely directed towards rearing those virtues which nature had planted with so liberal a hand in her children, and which, under the genial influence of her eye, had flourished and expanded into beauty and strength. A new hope, and new solicitudes, now arose in her breast; these dear children were arrived at an age, dangerous from its tender susceptibility, and from the influence which imagination has at that time over the passions. Impressions would soon be formed which would stamp their destiny for life. The anxious mother lived but in her children, and she had yet another cause of apprehension.

When Osbert learned the story of his father's death, his young heart glowed to avenge the deed. The late Earl, who had governed with the real dignity of power, was adored by his clan; they were eager to revenge his injuries; but oppressed by the generous compassion of the Countess, their murmurs sunk into silence: yet they fondly cherished the hope that their young Lord would one day lead them on to conquest and revenge. The time was now come when they looked to see this hope, the solace of many a cruel moment, realized. The tender fears of a mother would not suffer Matilda to risque* the chief of her last remaining comforts. She forbade Osbert to engage. He submitted in silence, and endeavoured by application to his favourite studies, to stifle the emotions which roused him to arms. He excelled in the various accomplishments of his rank, but chiefly in the martial exercises, for they were congenial to the nobility of his soul, and he had a secret pleasure in believing that they would one time assist him to do justice to the memory of his dead father. His warm imagination directed him to poetry, and he followed where she led. He loved to wander among the romantic scenes of the Highlands, where the wild variety of nature inspired him with all the enthusiasm of his favourite art.* He delighted in the terrible and in the grand, more than in the softer landscape; and, wrapt in the bright visions of fancy,* would often lose himself in awful solitudes.

It was in one of these rambles, that having strayed for some miles over hills covered with heath, from whence the eye was presented with only the bold outlines of uncultivated nature, rocks piled on rocks, cataracts and vast moors unmarked by the foot of traveller, he lost the path which he had himself made; he looked in vain for the objects which had directed him, and his heart, for the first time, felt the repulse of fear.* No vestige of a human being was to be seen, and the dreadful silence of the place was interrupted only by the roar of distant torrents, and by the screams of the birds which flew over his head. He shouted, and his voice was answered only by the deep echoes of the mountains. He remained for some time in a silent dread not wholly unpleasing, but which was soon heightened to a degree of terror not to be endured; and he turned his steps backward, forlorn, and dejected. His memory gave him back no image of the past; having wandered some time, he came to a narrow pass, which he entered, overcome with fatigue and fruitless search: he had not advanced far, when an abrupt opening in the rock suddenly presented him with a view of the most beautifully romantic spot he had ever seen. It was a valley almost surrounded by a barrier of wild rocks, whose base was shaded with thick woods of pine and fir. A torrent, which tumbled from the heights, and was seen between the woods, rushed with amazing impetuosity into a fine lake which flowed through the vale, and was lost in the deep recesses of the mountains. Herds of cattle grazed in the bottom, and the delighted eyes of Osbert were once more blessed with the sight of human dwellings. Far on the margin of the stream were scattered a few neat cottages.* His heart was so gladdened at the prospect, that he forgot he had yet the way to find which led to this Elysian vale.* He was just awakened to this distressing reality, when his attention was once more engaged by the manly figure of a young Highland peasant, who advanced towards him with an air of benevolence, and, having learned his distress, offered to conduct him to his cottage. Osbert accepted the invitation, and they wound down the hill, through an obscure and intricate path, together. They arrived at one of the cottages which the Earl had observed from the height; they entered, and the peasant presented his guest to a venerable old Highlander, his father. Refreshments were spread on the table by a pretty young girl, and Osbert, after having partook* of them and rested awhile, departed, accompanied by Alleyn, the young peasant, who had offered to be his guide. The length of the walk was beguiled by conversation. Osbert was interested by discovering in his companion a dignity of thought, and a course of sentiment similar to his own. On their way, they passed at some distance the castle of Dunbayne. This object gave to Osbert a bitter reflection, and drew from him a deep sigh. Alleyn made observations on the bad policy of oppression in a chief, and produced as an instance the Baron Malcolm. These lands, said he, are his, and they are scarcely sufficient to support his wretched people, who, sinking under severe exactions, suffer to lie uncultivated, tracts which would otherwise add riches to their Lord. His clan, oppressed by their burdens, threaten to rise and do justice to themselves by force of arms.* The Baron, in haughty confidence, laughs at their defiance, and is insensible to his danger: for should an insurrection happen, there are other clans who would eagerly join in his destruction, and punish with the same weapon the tyrant and the murderer. Surprised at the bold independence of these words, delivered with uncommon energy, the heart of Osbert beat quick, and 'O God! my father!' burst from his lips. Alleyn stood aghast! uncertain of the effect which his speech had produced; in an instant the whole truth flashed upon his mind: he beheld the son of the Lord whom he had been taught to love, and whose sad story had been impressed upon his heart in the early days of childhood; he sunk at his feet, and embraced his knees with a romantic ardor. The young Earl raised him from the ground, and the following words relieved him from his astonishment, and filled his eyes with tears of mingled joy and sorrow: 'There are other clans as ready as your own to avenge the wrongs of the noble Earl of Athlin; the Fitz-Henrys were ever friends to virtue.'* The countenance of the youth, while he spoke, was overspread with the glow of conscious dignity, and his eyes were animated with the pride of virtue.—The breast of Osbert kindled with the noble purpose, but the image of his weeping mother crossed his mind, and checked the ardor of the impulse. 'A time may come my friend,' said he, 'when your generous zeal will be accepted with the warmth of gratitude it deserves. Particular circumstances will not suffer me, at present, to say more.' The warm attachment of Alleyn to his father sunk deep in his heart.

It was evening before they reached the castle, and Alleyn remained the Earl's guest for that night.

CHAPTER II

THE following day was appointed for the celebration of an annual festival given by the Earl to his people, and he would not suffer Alleyn to depart. The hall was spread with tables; and dance and merriment resounded through the castle. It was usual on that day for the clan to assemble in arms, on account of an attempt, the memory of which it was meant to perpetuate, made, two centuries before, by an hostile clan to surprize them in their festivity.

In the morning were performed the martial exercises, in which emulation was excited by the honorary rewards bestowed on excellence. The Countess and her lovely daughter beheld, from the ramparts of the castle, the feats performed on the plains below. Their attention was engaged, and their curiosity excited by the appearance of a stranger who managed the lance and the bow with such exquisite dexterity, as to bear off each prize of chivalry.* It was Alleyn. He received the palm of victory, as was usual, from the hands of the Earl; and the modest dignity with which he accepted it, charmed the beholders.

The Earl honoured the feast with his presence, at the conclusion of which, each guest arose, and seizing his goblet with his left hand, and with his right striking his sword, drank to the memory of their departed Lord. The hall echoed with the general voice. Osbert felt it strike upon his heart the alarum of war. The people then joined hands, and drank to the honour of the son of their late master. Osbert understood the signal, and overcome with emotion, every consideration yielded to that of avenging his father. He arose, and harangued the clan with all the fire of youth and indignant virtue. As he spoke, the countenance of his people flashed with impatient joy; a deep murmur of applause ran through the assembly: and when he was silent each man, crossing his sword with that of his neighbour, swore by that sacred pledge of union, never to quit the cause in which they now engaged, till the life of their enemy had paid the debt of justice and of revenge.

In the evening, the wives and daughters of the peasantry came to the castle, and joined in the festivity. It was usual for the Countess and her ladies to observe from a gallery of the hall, the various performances of dance and song; and it had been a custom of old for the daughter of the castle to grace the occasion by performing a Scotch dance with the victor of the morning. This victor now was Alleyn, who beheld the lovely Mary led by the Earl into the hall, and presented to him as his partner in the dance. She received his homage with a sweet grace. She was dressed in the habit of a Highland lass,* and her fine auburn tresses, which waved in her neck, were ornamented only with a wreath of roses. She moved in the dance with the light steps of the Graces.* Profound silence reigned through the hall during the performance, and a soft murmur of applause arose on its conclusion. The admiration of the spectators was divided between Mary and the victorious stranger. She retired to the gallery, and the night concluded in joy to all but the Earl, and to Alleyn; but very different was the source and the complexion of their inquietude. The mind of Osbert revolved the chief occurrences of the day, and his soul burned with impatience to accomplish the purposes of filial piety; yet he dreaded the effect which the communication of his designs might have on the tender heart of Matilda: on the morrow, however, he resolved to acquaint her with them, and in a few days to rise and prosecute his cause with arms.

Alleyn, whose bosom, till now, had felt only for others' pains, began to be conscious of his own. His mind, uneasy and restless, gave him only the image of the high-born Mary; he endeavoured to exclude her idea, but with an effort so faint, that it would still intrude! Pleased, yet sad, he would not acknowledge, even to himself, that he loved; so ingenious are we to conceal every appearance of evil from ourselves. He arose with the dawn, and departed from the castle full of gratitude and secret love, to prepare his friends for the approaching war.

The Earl awoke from broken slumbers, and summoned all his fortitude to encounter the tender opposition of his mother. He entered her apartment with faultering steps, and his countenance betrayed the emotions of his soul. Matilda was soon informed of what her heart had foreboded, and overcome with dreadful sensation, sunk lifeless in her chair. Osbert flew to her assistance, and Mary and the attendants soon recovered her to sense and wretchedness.

The mind of Osbert was torn by the most cruel conflict: filial duty, honour, revenge, commanded him to go; filial love, regret, and pity, entreated him to stay. Mary fell at his feet, and clasping his knees with all the wild energy of grief besought him to relinquish his fatal purpose, and save his last surviving parent. Her tears, her sighs, and the soft simplicity of her air, spoke a yet stronger language than her tongue: but the silent grief of the Countess was still more touching, and in his endeavours to sooth her, he was on the point of yielding his resolution, when the figure of his dying father arose to his imagination, and stamped his purpose irrevocably.* The anxiety of a fond mother, presented Matilda with the image of her son bleeding and ghastly; and the death of her Lord was revived in her memory with all the agonizing grief that sad event had impressed upon her heart, the harsher characters of which, the lenient hand of time had almost obliterated. So lovely is Pity in all her attitudes, that fondness prompts us to believe she can never transgress; but she changes into a vice, when she overcomes the purposes of stronger virtue. Sterner principles now nerved the breast of Osbert against her influence and impelled him on to deeds of arms. He summoned a few of the most able and trusty of the clan, and held a council of war; in which it was resolved that Malcolm should be attacked with all the force they could assemble, and with all the speed which the importance of the preparation would allow. To prevent suspicion and alarm to the Baron, it was agreed it should be given out, that these preparations were intended for assistance to the Chief of a distant part. That when they set out on the expedition, they should pursue, for some time, a contrary way, but under favour of the night should suddenly change their route, and turn upon the castle of Dunbayne.

In the mean time, Alleyn was strenuous in exciting his friends to the cause, and so successful in the undertaking, as to have collected, in a few days, a number of no inconsiderable consequence. To the warm enthusiasm of virtue was now added a new motive of exertion. It was no longer simply an attachment to the cause of justice, which roused him to action; the pride of distinguishing himself in the eyes of his mistress, and of deserving her esteem by his zealous services, gave combined force to the first impulse of benevolence. The sweet thought of deserving her thanks, operated secretly on his soul, for he was yet ignorant of its influence there. In this state he again appeared at the castle, and told the Earl, that himself and his friends were ready to follow him whenever the signal should be given. His offer was accepted with the warmth of kindness it claimed, and he was desired to hold himself in readiness for the onset.

In a few days the preparations were completed, Alleyn and his friends were summoned, the clan assembled in arms,* and, with the young Earl at their head, departed on their expedition. The parting between Osbert and his family may be easily conceived; nor could all the pride of expected conquest suppress a sigh which escaped from Alleyn when his eyes bade adieu to Mary, who, with the Countess, stood on the terrace of the castle, pursuing with aching sight the march of her beloved brother, till distance veiled him from her view; she then turned into the castle weeping, and foreboding future calamity. She endeavoured, however, to assume an appearance of tranquillity, that she might deceive the fears of Matilda, and sooth her sorrow. Matilda, whose mind was strong as her heart was tender, since she could not prevent this hazardous undertaking, summoned all her fortitude to resist the impressions of fruitless grief, and to search for the good which the occasion might present. Her efforts were not vain; she found it in the prospect which the enterprize afforded of honour to the memory of her murdered Lord, and of retribution on the head of the murderer.

It was evening when the Earl departed from the castle; he pursued a contrary route till night favoured his designs, when he wheeled towards the castle of Dunbayne. The extreme darkness of the night assisted their plan, which was to scale the walls, surprize the centinels; burst their way into the inner courts sword in hand, and force the murderer from his retreat. They had trod many miles the dreary wilds, unassisted by the least gleam of light, when suddenly their ears were struck with the dismal note of a watch-bell, which chimed the hour of the night. Every heart beat to the sound. They knew they were near the abode of the Baron. They halted to consult concerning their proceedings, when it was agreed, that the Earl with Alleyn and a chosen few, should proceed to reconnoitre the castle, while the rest should remain at a small distance awaiting the signal of approach. The Earl and his party pursued their march with silent steps; they perceived a faint light, which they guessed to proceed from the watch-tower of the castle, and they were now almost under its walls. They paused awhile in silence to give breath to expectation, and to listen if any thing was stirring. All was involved in the gloom of night, and the silence of death prevailed. They had now time to examine, as well as the darkness would permit, the situation of the castle, and the height of the walls; and to prepare for the assault. The edifice was built with Gothic magnificence upon a high and dangerous rock.* Its lofty towers still frowned in proud sublimity, and the immensity of the pile stood a record of the ancient consequence of its possessors. The rock was surrounded by a ditch, broad, but not deep, over which were two draw-bridges, one on the north side, the other on the east; they were both up, but as they separated in the center, one half of the bridge remained on the side of the plains. The bridge on the north led to the grand gateway of the castle; that on the east to a small watch-tower: these were all the entrances. The rock was almost perpendicular with the walls, which were strong and lofty. After surveying the situation, they pitched upon a spot where the rock appeared most accessible, and which was contiguous to the principal gate, and gave signal to the clan. They approached in silence, and gently throwing down the bundles of faggot, which they had brought for the purpose, into the ditch, made themselves a bridge over which they passed in safety, and prepared to ascend the heights. It had been resolved that a party, of which Alleyn was one, should scale the walls, surprize the centinels, and open the gates to the rest of the clan, which, with the Earl, were to remain without. Alleyn was the first who fixed his ladder and mounted; he was instantly followed by the rest of his party, and with much difficulty, and some hazard, they gained the ramparts in safety. They traversed a part of the platform without hearing the sound of a voice or a step; profound sleep seemed to bury all. A number of the party approached some centinels who were asleep on their post; them they seized; while Alleyn, with a few others, flew to open the nearest gate, and to let down the draw-bridge. This they accomplished; but in the mean time the signal of surprize was given, and instantly the alarm bell rang out, and the castle resounded with the clang of arms. All was tumult and confusion. The Earl, with part of his people, entered the gate; the rest were following, when suddenly the portcullis was dropped, the bridge drawn up, and the Earl and his people found themselves surrounded by an armed multitude, which poured in torrents from every recess of the castle. Surprized, but not daunted, the Earl rushed forward sword in hand, and fought with a desperate valour. The soul of Alleyn seemed to acquire new vigour from the conflict; he fought like a man panting for honour, and certain of victory; wherever he rushed, conquest flew before him. He, with the Earl, forced his way into the inner courts, in search of the Baron, and hoped to have satisfied a just revenge, and to have concluded the conflict with the death of the murderer; but the moment in which they entered the courts, the gates were closed upon them; they were environed by a band of guards; and, after a short resistance, in which Alleyn received a slight wound, they were seized as prisoners of war. The slaughter without was great and dreadful: the people of the Baron inspired with fury, were insatiate for death: many of the Earl's followers were killed in the courts and on the platform; many, in attempting to escape, were thrown from the ramparts, and many were destroyed by the sudden raising of the bridge. A small part, only of the brave and adventurous band who had engaged in the cause of justice, and who were driven back from the walls, survived to carry the dreadful tidings to the Countess. The fate of the Earl remained unknown. The consternation among the friends of the slain is not to be described, and it was heightened by the unaccountable manner in which the victory had been obtained; for it was well known that Malcolm had never, but when war made it necessary, more soldiers in his garrison than feudal pomp demanded; yet on this occasion, a number of armed men rushed from the recesses of his castle, sufficient to overpower the force of a whole clan. But they knew not the secret means of intelligence which the Baron possessed; the jealousy of conscience had armed him with apprehension for his safety; and for some years he had planted spies near the castle of Athlin, to observe all that passed within it, and to give him immediate intelligence of every war-like preparation. A transaction so striking, and so public as that which had occurred on the day of the festival, when the whole people swore to avenge the murder of their Chief, it was not probable would escape the vigilant eye of his mercenaries: the circumstance had been communicated to him with all the exaggerations of fear and wonder, and had given him the signal for defence. The accounts sent him of the military preparations which were forming, convinced him that this defence would soon be called for; and, laughing at the idle tales which were told him of distant wars, he hastened to store his garrison with arms and with men, and held himself in readiness to receive the assailants. The Baron had conducted his plans with all that power of contrivance which the secrecy of the business demanded; and it was his design to suffer the enemy to mount his walls, and to put them to the sword, when the purpose of this deep-laid stratagem had been nearly defeated by the drowsiness of the centinels who were posted to give signal of their approach.

The fortitude of Matilda fainted under the pressure of so heavy a calamity; she was attacked with a violent illness, which had nearly terminated her sorrows and her life; and had rendered unavailing all the tender cares of her daughter. These tender cares, however, were not ineffectual; she revived, and they assisted to support her in the severe hours of affliction, which the unknown fate of the Earl occasioned. Mary, who felt all the horrors of the late event, was ill qualified for the office of a comforter; but her generous heart, susceptible of the deep sufferings of Matilda, almost forgot its own distress in the remembrance of her mother's. Yet the idea of her brother, surrounded with the horrors of imprisonment and death, would often obtrude itself on her imagination, with an emphasis which almost overcame her reason. She had also a strong degree of pity for the fate of the brave young Highlander who had assisted, with a disinterestedness so noble, in the cause of her house; she wished to learn his further destiny, and her heart often melted in compassion at the picture which her fancy drew of his sufferings.

CHAPTER III

THE Earl, after being loaded with fetters, was conducted to the chief prison of the castle, and left alone to the bitter reflections of defeat and uncertain destiny; but misfortune, though it might shake, could not overcome his firmness; and hope had not yet entirely forsaken him. It is the peculiar attribute of great minds, to bear up with encreasing force against the shock of misfortune; with them the nerves of resistance strengthen with attack; and they may be said to subdue adversity with her own weapons.

Reflection, at length, afforded him time to examine his prison: it was a square room, which formed the summit of a tower built on the east side of the castle, round which the bleak winds howled mournfully; the inside of the apartment was old and falling to decay: a small mattrass,* which lay in one corner of the room, a broken matted chair, and a tottering table, composed its furniture; two small and strongly grated windows, which admitted a sufficient degree of light and air, afforded him on one side a view into an inner court, and on the other a dreary prospect of the wild and barren Highlands.

Alleyn was conveyed through dark and winding passages to a distant part of the castle, where at length a small door, barred with iron, opened, and disclosed to him an abode, whence light and hope were equally excluded. He shuddered as he entered, and the door was closed upon him.

The mind of the Baron, in the mean time, was agitated with all the direful passions of hate, revenge, and exulting pride. He racked imagination for the invention of tortures equal to the force of his feelings; and he at length discovered that the sufferings of suspense are superior to those of the most terrible evils, when once ascertained, of which the contemplation gradually affords to strong minds the means of endurance.* He determined, therefore, that the Earl should remain confined in the tower, ignorant of his future destiny; and in the mean while should be allowed food only sufficient to keep him sensible of his wretchedness.

Osbert was immersed in thought, when he heard the door of

his prison unbarred, and the Baron Malcolm stood before him. The heart of Osbert swelled high with indignation, and defiance flashed in his eyes. 'I am come,' said the insulting victor, 'to welcome the Earl of Athlin to my castle; and to shew that I can receive my friends with the hospitality they deserve; but I am yet undetermined what kind of festival I shall bestow on his arrival.'

'Weak tyrant,' returned Osbert, his countenance impressed with the firm dignity of virtue, 'to insult the vanquished, is congenial with the cruel meanness of the murderer; nor do I expect, that the man who slew the father, will spare the son; but know, that son is nerved against your wrath, and welcomes all that your fears or your cruelty can impose.'

'Rash youth,' replied the Baron; 'your words are air; they fade from sense, and soon your boasted strength shall sink beneath my power. I go to meditate your destiny.' With these words he quitted the prison, enraged at the unbending virtue of the Earl.

The sight of the Baron, roused in the soul of Osbert all those opposite emotions of furious indignation and tender pity which the glowing image of his father could excite, and produced a moment of perfect misery. The dreadful energy of these sensations exasperated his brain almost to madness; the cool fortitude in which he had so lately gloried, disappeared; and he was on the point of resigning his virtue and his life, by means of a short dagger,* which he wore concealed under his vest, when the soft notes of a lute* surprised his attention. It was accompanied by a voice so enchantingly tender and melodious, that its sounds fell on the heart of Osbert in balmy comfort: it seemed sent by Heaven to arrest his fate:—the storm of passion was hushed within him, and he dissolved in kind tears of pity and contrition. The mournful tenderness of the air declared the person from whom it came to be a sufferer; and Osbert suspected it to proceed from a prisoner like himself. The music ceased. Absorbed in wonder, he went to the grates, in quest of the sweet musician, but no one was to be seen; and he was uncertain whether the sounds arose from within or from without the castle. Of the guard, who brought him his small allowance of food, he inquired concerning what he had heard; but from him he could not obtain the information he sought, and he was constrained to remain in a state of suspense.

In the mean time the castle of Athlin, and its neighbourhood, was overwhelmed with distress. The news of the earl's imprisonment at length reached the ears of the countess, and hope once more illumined her mind. She immediately sent offers of immense ransom to the baron, for the restoration of her son, and the other prisoners; but the ferocity of his nature disdained an incomplete triumph. Revenge subdued his avarice; and the offers were rejected with the spurn of contempt. An additional motive, however, operated in his mind, and confirmed his purpose. The beauty of Mary had been often reported to him in terms which excited his curiosity; and an incidental view he once obtained of her, raised a passion in his soul, which the turbulence of his character would not suffer to be extinguished. Various were the schemes he had projected to obtain her, none of which had ever been executed: the possession of the earl was a circumstance the most favourable to his wishes; and he resolved to obtain Mary, as the future ransom of her brother. He concealed, for the present, his purpose, that the tortures of anxiety and despair might operate on the mind of the countess, to grant him an easy consent to the exchange, and to resign the victim the wife of her enemy.

The small remains of the clan, unsubdued by misfortune, were eager to assemble; and, hazardous as was the enterprize, to attempt the rescue of their Chief. The hope which this undertaking afforded, once more revived the Countess; but alas! a new source of sorrow was now opened for her: the health of Mary visibly declined; she was silent and pensive; her tender frame was too susceptible of the s...ferings of her mind; and these sufferings were heightened by concealment. She was prescribed amusement and gentle exercise, as the best restoratives of peace and health. One day, as she was seeking on horseback these lost treasures, she was tempted by the fineness of the evening to prolong her ride beyond its usual limits: the sun was declining when she entered a wood, whose awful glooms so well accorded with the persive tone of her mind. The soft serenity of evening, and the still solemnity of the scene, conspired to lull her mind into a pleasing forgetfulness of its troubles; from which she was, ere long, awakened by the approaching sound of horses' feet. The thickness of the foliage limited her view; but looking onward, she thought she perceived through the trees, a glittering of arms; she turned her palfry,* and sought the entrance of the wood. The clattering of hoofs advanced in the breeze! her heart misgave her, and she quickened her pace. Her fears were soon justified; she looked back, and beheld three horsemen armed and disguised advancing with the speed of pursuit. Almost fainting, she flew on the wings of terror; all her efforts were vain; the villains came up; one seized her horse, the others fell upon her two attendants: a stout scuffle ensued, but the strength of her servants soon yielded to the weapons of their adversaries; they were brought to the ground, dragged into the wood, and there left bound to the trees. In the mean time, Mary, who had fainted in the arms of the villain who seized her, was borne away through the intricate mazes of the woods; and her terrors may be easily imagined, when she revived, and found herself in the hands of unknown men. Her dreadful screams, her tears, her supplications, were ineffectual; the wretches were deaf alike to pity and to enquiry; they preserved an inflexible silence, and she saw herself conveying towards the mouth of a horrible cavern, when despair seized her mind, and she lost all signs of existence: in this state she remained some time; but it is impossible to describe her situation, when she unclosed her eyes, and beheld Alleyn, who was watching with the most trembling anxiety her return to life, and whose eyes, on seeing her revive, swam in joy and tenderness.* Wonder, fearful joy, and the various shades of mingled emotions, passed in quick succession over her countenance; her surprize was increased, when she observed her own servants standing by, and could discover no one but friends. She scarcely dared to trust her senses, but the voice of Alleyn, tremulous with tenderness, dissolved in a moment the illusions of fear, and confirmed her in the surprising reality. When she was sufficiently recovered, they quitted this scene of gloom: they travelled on in a slow pace, and the shades of night were fallen long before they reached the castle; there distress and confusion appeared. The Countess, alarmed with the most dreadful apprehensions, had dispatched her servants various ways in search of her child, and her transports on again beholding her in safety, prevented her observing immediately that it was Alleyn who accompanied her. Joy, however, soon yielded to its equal wonder, when she perceived him, and in the tumult of contending emotions, she scarce knew which first to interrogate. When she had been told the escape of her daughter, and by whom effected, she prepared to hear, with impatient solicitude, news of her beloved son, and the means by which the brave young Highlander had eluded the vigilance of the Baron. Of the Earl, Alleyn could only inform the Countess, that he was taken prisoner with himself, within the walls of the fortress, as they fought side by side; that he was conducted unwounded, to a tower, situated on the east angle of the castle, where he was still confined. Himself had been imprisoned in a distant part of the pile, and had been able to collect no other particulars of the Earl's situation, than those he had related. Of himself he gave a brief relation of the following circumstances:

After having lain some weeks in the horrible dungeon allotted him, his mind involved in the gloom of despair, and filled with the momentary expectation of death, desperation furnished him with invention, and he concerted the following plan of escape:— He had observed, that the guard who brought him his allowance of food, on quitting the dungeon, constantly sounded his spear against the pavement near the entrance. This circumstance excited his surprize and curiosity. A ray of hope beamed through the gloom of his dungeon. He examined the spot, as well as the obscurity of the place would permit; it was paved with flag stones like the other parts of the cell, and the paving was every where equally firm. He, however, became certain, that some means of escape was concealed beneath that part, for the guard was constant in examining it by striking that spot, and treading more firmly on it; and this he endeavoured to do without being observed. One day, immediately after the departure of the guard, Alleyn set himself to unfasten the pavement; this, with much patience and industry, he effected, by means of a small knife which had escaped the search of the soldiers. He found the earth beneath hard, and without any symptoms of being lately disturbed; but after digging a few feet, he arrived at a trap door; he trembled with eagerness. It was now almost night, and he was overcome with weariness; he doubted whether he should be able to penetrate through the door, and what other obstructions were behind it, before the next day. He therefore, threw the earth again into the hole, and endeavoured to close the pavement; with much difficulty, he trod the earth into the opening, but the pavement he was unable exactly to replace. It was too dark to examine the stones; and he found, that even if he should be able to make them fit, the pavement could not be made firm. His mind and body were now overcome, and he threw himself on the ground in an agony of despair. It was midnight, when the return of his strength and spirits produced another effort. He tore the earth up with hasty violence, cut round the lock of the trap door, and raising it, unwilling to hesitate or consider, sprung through the aperture. The vault was of considerable depth, and he was thrown down by the violence of the fall: an hollow echo, which seemed to murmur at a distance, convinced him that the place was of considerable extent. He had no light to direct him, and was therefore obliged to walk with his arms extended, in silent and fearful examination. After having wandered through the void a considerable time, he came to a wall, along which he groped with anxious care; it conducted him onward for a length of way: it turned; he followed, and his hand touched the cold iron work of a barred window. He felt the gentle undulation of the air upon his face; and to him, who had been so long confined among the damp vapours of a dungeon, this was a moment of luxury. The air gave him strength; and the means of escape, which now seemed presented to him, renewed his courage. He set his foot against the wall, and grasping a bar with his hand, found it gradually yield to his strength, and by successive efforts, he entirely displaced it. He attempted another but, it was more firmly fixed, and every effort to loosen it was ineffectual; he found that it was fastened in a large stone of the wall, and to remove this stone, was his only means of displacing the bar; he set himself, therefore, again to work with his knife, and with much patience, loosened the mortar sufficiently to effect his purpose. After some hours, for the darkness made his labour tedious, and sometimes ineffectual, he had removed several of the bars, and had made an opening almost sufficient to permit his escape, when the dawn of light appeared; he now discovered, with inexpressible anguish, that the grate opened into an inner court of the castle, and even while he hesitated, he could perceive soldiers descending slowly into the court, from the narrow staircases which led to their apartments. His heart sickened at the sight. He rested against the wall in a pause of despair, and was on the point of springing into the court, to make a desperate effort at escape, or die in the attempt, when he perceived, by the encreasing light which fell across the vault, a massy door in the wall; he ran towards it, and endeavoured to open it; it was fastened by a lock and several bolts. He struck against it with his foot, and the hollow sound which was returned, convinced him that there were vaults beyond; and by the direction of these vaults, he was certain that they must extend to the outer walls of the castle; if he could gain these vaults, and penetrate beyond them in the darkness of the ensuing night, it would be easy to leap the wall, and cross the ditch; but it was impossible to cut away the lock, before the return of his guard, who regularly visited the cell soon after the dawn of day. After some consideration, therefore, he determined to secrete himself in a dark part of the vault, and there await the entrance of the guard, who on observing the deranged bars of the grate, would conclude, that he had escaped through the aperture. He had scarcely placed himself according to his plan, when he heard the door of the dungeon unbolted; this was instantly followed by a loud voice, which founded down the opening, and 'Alleyn' was shouted in a tone of fright and consternation. After repeating the call, a man jumped into the vault. Alleyn, though himself concealed in darkness, could perceive, by the faint light which fell upon the spot, a soldier with a drawn sword in his hand. He approached the grate with execrations, examined it, and proceeded to the door; it was fast, he returned to the grate, and then proceeded along the walls, tracing them with the point of his sword. He at length approached the spot where Alleyn was concealed, who felt the sword strike upon his arm, and instantly grasping the hand which held it, the weapon fell to the ground. A short scuffle ensued. Alleyn threw down his adversary, and standing over him, seized the sword, and presented it to his breast; the soldier called for mercy. Alleyn, always unwilling to take the life of another, and considering that if the soldier was slain, his comrades would certainly follow to the vault, returned him his sword. 'Take your life,' said he, 'your death can avail me nothing;—take it, and if you can, go tell Malcolm, that an innocent man has endeavoured to escape destruction.' The guard, struck with his conduct, arose from the ground in silence, he received his sword, and followed Alleyn to the trap door. They returned into the dungeon, where Alleyn was once more left alone. The soldier, undetermined how to act, went to find his comrades; on the way he met Malcolm, who, ever restless and vigilant frequently walked the ramparts at an early hour. He enquired if all was well. The soldier, fearful of discovery, and unaccustomed to dissemble, hesitated at the question; and the stern air assumed by Malcolm, compelled him to relate what had happened. The Baron, with much harshness, reprobated his neglect, and immediately followed him to the dungeon, where he loaded Alleyn with insult. He examined the cell, descended into the vault, and returning to the dungeon stood by, while a chain, which had been fetched from a distant part of the castle, was fixed into the wall;—to this Alleyn was fastened. 'We will not long confine you thus,' said Malcolm as he quitted the cell, 'a few days shall restore you to the liberty you are so fond of; but as a conqueror ought to have spectators of his triumph, you must wait till a number is collected sufficient to witness the death of so great an hero.' 'I disdain your insults,' returned Alleyn, 'and am equally able to support misfortune, and to despise a tyrant.' Malcolm retired enraged at the boldness of his prisoner, and uttering menaces on the carelessness of the guard, who vainly endeavoured to justify himself. 'His safety be upon your head,' said the Baron. The soldier was shocked, and turned away in sullen silence. Dread of his prisoner's effecting an escape, now seized his mind; the words of Malcolm filled him with resentment, while gratitude towards Alleyn, for the life he had spared, operated with these sentiments, and he hesitated whether he should obey the Baron, or deliver Alleyn, and fly his oppressor.

At noon, he carried him his customary food; Alleyn was not so lost in misery, but that he observed the gloom which hung upon his features; his heart foreboded impending evil: the soldier bore on his tongue the sentence of death. He told Alleyn, that the Baron had appointed the following day for his execution; and his people were ordered to attend. Death, however long contemplated, must be dreadful when it arrives; this was no more than what Alleyn had expected, and on what he had brought his mind to gaze without terror; but his fortitude now sunk before its immediate presence, and every nerve of his frame thrilled with agony. 'Be comforted,' said the soldier, in a tone of pity, 'I, too, am no stranger to misery; and if you are willing to risque the danger of double torture, I will attempt to release both you and myself from the hands of a tyrant.' At these words, Alleyn started from the ground in a transport of delightful wonder: 'Tell me not of torture,' cried he, 'all tortures are equal if death is the end, and from death I may now escape; lead me but beyond these walls, and the small possessions I have, shall be yours for ever.' 'I want them not,' replied the generous soldier, 'it is enough for me, that I save a fellow creature from destruction.' These words overpowered the heart of Alleyn, and tears of gratitude swelled in his eyes. Edric told him, that the door he had seen in the vault below, opened into a chain of vaults, which stretched beyond the wall of the castle, and communicated with a subterraneous way, anciently formed as a retreat from the fortress, and which terminated in the cavern of a forest at some distance.* If this door could be opened, their escape was almost certain. They consulted on the measures necessary to be taken. The soldier gave Alleyn a knife larger than the one he had, and directed him to cut round the lock, which was all that with-held their passage.—Edric's office of centinel was propitious to their scheme, and it was agreed that at midnight they should descend the vaults. Edric, after having unfastened the chain, left the cell, and Alleyn set himself again to remove the pavement, which had been already re-placed by order of the Baron. The near prospect of deliverance now gladdened his spirits; his knife was better formed for his purpose; and he worked with alacrity and ease. He arrived at the trap door, and once more leaped into the vault.

He applied himself to the lock of the door, which was extremely thick, and it was with difficulty he separated them; with trembling hands he undrew the bolts, the door unclosed, and discovered to him the vaults. It was evening when he finished his work. He was but just returned to the dungeon, and had thrown himself on the ground to rest, when the sound of a distant step caught his ear; he listened to its advance with trembling eagerness. At length the door was unbolted; Alleyn, breathless with expectation, started up, and beheld not his soldier, but another; the opening was again discovered, and all was now over. The soldier brought a pitcher of water, and casting round the place a look of sullen scrutiny, departed in silence. The stretch of human endurance was now exceeded, and Alleyn sunk down in a state of torpidity. On recovering, he found himself again enveloped in the horrors of darkness, silence, and despair. Yet amid all his sufferings, he disdained to doubt the integrity of his soldier: we naturally recoil from painful sensations, and it is one of the most exquisite tortures of a noble mind, to doubt the sincerity of those in whom it has confided. Alleyn concluded, that the conversation of the morning had been overheard, and that this guard had been sent to examine the cell, and to watch his movements. He believed that Edric was now, by his own generosity, involved in destruction; and in the energy of this thought, he forgot for a moment his own situation.

Midnight came, but Edric did not appear; his doubts were now confirmed into certainty, and he resigned himself to the horrid tranquillity of mute despair. He heard, from a distance, the clock of the castle strike one; it seemed to sound the knell of death; it roused his benumbed senses, and he rose from the ground in an agony of acutest recollection. Suddenly he heard the steps of two persons advancing down the avenue; he started, and listened. Malcolm and murder arose to his mind; he doubted not that the soldier had reported what he had seen in the evening, and that the persons whom he now heard, were coming to execute the final orders of the Baron. They now drew near the dungeon, when suddenly he remembered the door in the vault. His senses had been so stunned by the appearance of the stranger, and his mind so occupied with a feeling of despair, as to exclude every idea of escape; and in the energy of his sufferings he had forgot this last resource. It now flashed like lightning upon his mind; he sprung to the trap door, and his feet had scarcely touched the bottom of the vault, when he heard the bolts of the dungeon undraw; he had just reached the entrance of the inner vault, when a voice sounded from above. He paused, and knew it to be Edric's. Apprehension so entirely possessed his mind, that he hesitated whether he should discover himself; but a moment of recollection dissipated every ignoble suspicion of Edric's fidelity, and he answered the call. Immediately Edric descended, followed by the soldier whose former appearance had filled Alleyn with despair, and whom Edric now introduced as his faithful friend and comrade, who, like himself, was weary of the oppression of Malcolm, and who had resolved to fly with them, and escape his rigour. This was a moment of happiness too great for thought! Alleyn, in the confusion of his joy, and in his impatience to seize the moment of deliverance, scarcely heard the words of Edric. Edric having returned to fasten the door of the dungeon, to delay pursuit, and given Alleyn a sword which he had brought for him, led the way through the vaults. The profound silence of the place was interrupted only by the echoes of their footsteps, which running through the dreary chasms in confused whisperings, filled their imaginations with terror. In traversing these gloomy and desolate recesses they often paused to listen, and often did their fears give them the distant sounds of pursuit. On quitting the vaults, they entered an avenue, winding, and of considerable length, from whence branched several passages into the rock. It was closed by a low and narrow door, which opened upon a flight of steps, that led to the subterraneous way under the ditch of the castle. Edric knew the intricacies of the place: they entered, and closing the door began to descend, when the lamp which Edric carried in his hand was blown out by the current of the wind, and they were left in total darkness. Their feelings may be more easily imagined than described; they had, however, no way but to proceed, and grope with cautious steps the dark abyss. Having continued to descend for some time, their feet reached the bottom, and they found themselves once more on even ground; but Edric knew they had yet another flight to encounter, before they could gain the subterraneous passage under the fosse,* and for which it required their utmost caution to search. They were proceeding with slow and wary steps, when the foot of Alleyn stumbled upon something which clattered like broken armour, and endeavouring to throw it from him, he felt the weight resist his effort: he stooped to discover what it was, and found in his grasp the cold hand of a dead person. Every nerve thrilled with horror at the touch, and he started back in an agony of terror. They remained for some time in silent dismay, unable to return, yet fearful to proceed, when a faint light which seemed to issue from the bottom of the last descent, gleamed upon the walls, and discovered to them the second staircase, and at their feet the pale and disfigured corpse of a man in armour, while at a distance they could distinguish the figures of men. At this sight their hearts died within them, and they gave themselves up for lost. They doubted not but the men whom they saw were the murderers; that they belonged to the Baron; and were in search of some fugitives from the castle. Their only chance of concealment was to remain where they were; but the light appeared to advance, and the faces of the men to turn towards them. Winged with terror, they sought the first ascent, and flying up the steps, reached the door, which they endeavoured to open, that they might hide themselves from pursuit among the intricacies of the rock; their efforts, however, were vain, for the door was fastened by a spring lock, and the key was on the other side. Compelled to give breath to their fears, they ventured to look back, and found themselves again in total darkness; they paused upon the steps, and listening, all was silent. They rested here a considerable time; no footsteps startled them; no ray of light darted through the gloom; every thing seemed hushed in the silence of death: they resolved once more to venture forward; they gained again the bottom of the first descent, and shuddering as they approached the spot where they knew the corpse was laid, they groped to avoid its horrid touch, when suddenly the light again appeared, and in the same place where they had first seen it. They stood petrified with despair. The light, however, moved slowly onward, and disappeared in the windings of the avenue. After remaining a long time in silent suspense, and finding no further obstacle, they ventured to proceed. The light had discovered to them their situation, and the staircase, and they now moved with greater certainty. They reached the bottom in safety, and without any fearful interruption; they listened, and again the silence of the place was undisturbed. Edric knew they were now under the fosse, their way was plain before them, and their hopes were renewed in the belief, that the light and the people they had seen, had taken a different direction, Edric knowing there were various passages branching from the main avenue which led to different openings in the rock. They now stepped on with alacrity, the prospect of deliverance was near, for Edric judged they were now not far from the cavern. An abrupt turning in the passage confirmed at once this supposition, and extinguished the hope which had attended it; for the light of a lamp burst suddenly upon them, and exhibited to their sickening eyes, the figures of four men in an attitude of menace, with their swords pointed ready to receive them. Alleyn drew his sword, and advanced: 'We will die hardly,' cried he. At the sound of his voice, the weapons instantly dropped from the hands of his adversaries, and they advanced to meet him in a transport of joy. Alleyn recognized with astonishment, in the faces of the three strangers, his faithful friends and followers; and Edric in that of the fourth, a fellow soldier. The same purpose had assembled them all in the same spot. They quitted the cave together; and Alleyn, in the joyful experience of unexpected deliverance, resolved never more to admit despair. They concluded, that the body which they had passed in the avenue, was that of some person who had perished either by hunger or by the sword in those subterranean labyrinths.

They marched in company till they came within a few miles of the castle of Athlin, when Alleyn made known his design of collecting his friends, and joining the clan in an attempt to release the Earl; Edric, and the other soldier, having solemnly enlisted in the cause, they parted; Alleyn and Edric pursuing the road to the castle, and the others striking off to a different part of the country. Alleyn and Edric had not proceeded far, when the groans of the wounded servants of Matilda drew them into the wood, in which the preceding dreadful scene had been acted. The surprize of Alleyn was extreme, when he discovered the servants of the Earl in this situation; but surprize soon yielded to a more poignant sensation, when he heard that Mary had been carried off by armed men. He scarcely waited to release the servants, but seized one of their horses which was grazing near, instantly mounted, ordering the rest to follow, and took the way which had been pointed as the course of the ravishers. Fortunately it was the right direction; and Alleyn and the soldier came up with them as they were hastening to the mouth of that cavern, whose frightful aspect had chilled the heart of Mary with a temporary death. Their endeavours to fly were vain; they were overtaken at the entrance; a sharp conflict ensued in which one of the ruffians was wounded and fled: his comrades seeing the servants of the Earl approaching relinquished their prize, and escaped through the recesses of the cave. The eyes of Alleyn were now fixed in horror on the lifeless form of Mary, who had remained insensible during the whole of the affray; he was exerting every effort for her recovery, when she unclosed her eyes, and joy once more illumined his soul.

During the recital of these particulars, which Alleyn delivered with a modest brevity, the mind of Mary had suffered a variety of emotions sympathetic to all the vicissitudes of his situation. She endeavoured to conceal from herself the particular interest she felt in his adventures; but so unequal were her efforts to the strength of her emotions, that when Alleyn related the scene of Dunbayne cavern, her cheek grew pale and she relapsed into a fainting fit. This circumstance alarmed the penetration of the Countess; but the known weakness of her daughter's frame appeared a probable cause of the disorder, and repressed her first apprehension. It gave to Alleyn a mixed delight of hope and fear, such as he had never known before; for the first time he dared to acknowledge to his own heart that he loved, and that heart for the first time thrilled with the hope of being loved again.

He received from the Countess the warm overflowings of a heart grateful for the preservation of her child, and from Mary a blush which spoke more than her tongue could utter. But the minds of all were involved in the utmost perplexity concerning the rank and the identity of the author of the plan, nor could they discover any clue which would lead them through this intricate maze of wonder, to the villain who had fabricated so diabolical a scheme. Their suspicions, at length, rested upon the Baron Malcolm, and this supposition was confirmed by the appearance of the horsemen, who evidently acted only as the agents of superior power. Their conjectures were indeed just. Malcolm was the author of the scheme. It had been planned, and he had given orders to his people to execute it long before the Earl fell into his hands. They had, however, found no opportunity of accomplishing the design when the castle was surprised, and in the consequent tumult of his mind, the Baron had forgot to withdraw his orders.

Alleyn expressed his design of collecting the small remnant of his friends, and uniting with the clan in attempting the rescue of the Earl. 'Noble youth,' exclaimed the Countess, unable longer to repress her admiration, 'how can I ever repay your generous services! Am I then to receive both my children at your hands? Go—my clan are now collecting for a second attempt upon the walls of Dunbayne,—go! lead them to conquest, and restore to me my son.' The languid eyes of Mary rekindled at these words, she glowed with the hope of clasping once more to her bosom her long lost brother; but the suffusions of hope were soon chaced by the chilly touch of fear, for it was Alleyn who was to lead the enterprize, and it was Alleyn who might fall in the attempt. These contrary emotions unveiled to her at once the state of her affections, and she saw in the eye of fancy, the long train of inquietudes and sorrows which were likely to ensue. She sought to obliterate from her mind every remembrance of the past, and of the fatal knowledge which was now disclosed; but she sought in vain, for the monitor* in her breast constantly presented to her mind the image of Alleyn, adorned with those brave and manly virtues which had so eminently distinguished his conduct; the insignificance of the peasant was lost in the nobility of the character, and every effort at forgetfulness was baffled.

Alleyn passed that night at the castle, and the next morning, after taking leave of the Countess and her daughter, to whom his eyes bade a respectful and mournful adieu, he departed with Edric for his father's cottage, impatient to acquaint the good old man with his safety, and to rouse to arms his slumbering friends. The breath of love had now raised into flame those sparks of ambition which had so long been kindling in his breast; he was not only eager to avenge the cause of injured virtue, and to rescue from misery and death, the son of the Chief whom he had been ever taught to reverence, but he panted to avenge the insult offered to his mistress, and to achieve some deed of valour worthy her admiration and her thanks.

Alleyn found his father at breakfast, with his niece at his side; his face was darkened with sorrow, and he did not perceive Alleyn, when he entered. The joy of the old man almost overcame him when he beheld his son in safety, for he was the solace of his declining years; and Edric was welcomed with the heartiness of an old friend.

CHAPTER IV

MEANWHILE the Earl remained a solitary prisoner in the tower; uncertain fate was yet suspended over him; he had, however, a magnanimity in his nature which baffled much of the cruel effort of the Baron. He had prepared his mind by habitual contemplation for the worst, and although that worst was death, he could now look to it even with serenity. Those violent transports which had assailed him on sight of the Baron, were, since he was no longer subject to his presence, reduced within their proper limits; yet he anxiously avoided dwelling on the memory of his father, lest those dreadful sensations should threaten him with returning torture. Whenever he permitted himself to think of the sufferings of the Countess and his sister, his heart melted with a sorrow that almost unnerved him; much he wished to know how they supported this trial, and much he wished that he could convey to them intelligence of his state. He endeavoured to abstract his mind from his situation, and sought to make himself artificial comforts even from the barren objects around him; his chief amusement was in observing the manners and customs of the birds of prey which lodged themselves in the battlements of his tower, and the rapacity of their nature furnished him with too just a parallel to the habits of men.

As he was one day standing at the grate which looked upon the castle, observing the progress of these birds, his ear caught the sound of that sweet lute whose notes had once saved him from destruction; it was accompanied by the same melodious voice he had formerly heard, and which now sung with impassioned tenderness the following air:

> When first the vernal morn of life*
> Beam'd on my infant eye,
> Fond I survey'd the smiling scene,
> Nor saw the tempest nigh.
>
> Hope's bright illusions touch'd my soul,
> My young ideas led;

And Fancy's vivid tints combin'd,
  And fairy prospect spread.

My guileless heart expanded wide,
  With filial fondness fraught;
Paternal love that heart supplied
  With all its fondness sought.

But O! the cruel quick reverse!
  Fate all I loved involv'd;
Pale Grief Hope's trembling rays dispers'd,
  And Fancy's dreams dissolv'd.

Lost in surprize, Osbert stood for some time looking down upon an inner court, whence the sounds seemed to arise; after a few minutes he observed a young lady enter from that side on which the tower arose; on her arm rested an elder one, in whose face might be traced the lines of decaying beauty; but it was visible, from the melancholy which clouded her features, that the finger of affliction had there anticipated the ravages of time. She was dressed in the habit of a widow, and the black veil which shaded her forehead, and gave a fine expression to her countenance, devolved upon the ground in a length of train, and heightened the natural majesty of her figure; she moved with slow steps, and was supported by the young lady whose veil half disclosed a countenance where beauty was touched with sorrow and inimitable expression; the elegance of her form and the dignity of her air, proclaimed her to be of distinguished rank. On her arm was hung that lute, whose melody had just charmed the attention of the Earl, who was now fixed in wonder at what he beheld, that was equalled only by his admiration. They retired through a gate on the opposite side of the court, and were seen no more. Osbert followed them with his eyes, which for some time remained fixed upon the door through which they had disappeared, almost insensible of their departure. When he returned to himself, he discovered, as if for the first time, that he was in solitude. He conjectured that these strangers were confined by the oppressive power of the Baron, and his eyes were suffused with tears of pity. When he considered that so much beauty and dignity were the unresisting victims of a tyrant, his heart swelled high with indignation, his prison became intolerable to him, and he longed to become at once the champion of virtue,* and the deliverer of oppressed innocence. The character of Malcolm arose to his mind black with accumulated guilt, and aggravated the detestation with which he had ever contemplated it: the hateful idea nerved his soul with a confidence of revenge. Of the guard, who entered, he enquired concerning the strangers, but could obtain no positive information; he came to impart other news; to prepare the Earl for death; the morrow was appointed for his execution. He received the intelligence with the firm hardihood of indignant virtue, disdaining to solicit, and disdaining to repine; and his mind yet grasped the idea of revenge. He drove from his thoughts, with precipitation, the tender ideas of his mother and sister; remembrances which would subdue his fortitude without effecting any beneficial purpose. He was told of the escape of Alleyn; this intelligence gave him inexpressible pleasure, and he knew this faithful youth would undertake to avenge his death.

When the news of Alleyn's flight had reached the Baron, his soul was stung with rage, and he called for the guards of the dungeon; they were no where to be found; and after a long search it was known that they were fled with their prisoner; the flight of the other captives was also discovered. This circumstance exasperated the passion of Malcolm to the utmost, and he gave orders that the life of the remaining centinel should be forfeited for the treachery of his comrades, and his own negligence; when recollecting the Earl, whom in the heat of his resentment he had forgot, his heart exulted in the opportunity he afforded of complete revenge; and in the fullness of joy with which he pronounced his sentence, he retracted the condemnation of the trembling guard. The moment after he had dispatched the messenger with his resolve to the Earl, his heart faultered from its purpose. Such is the alternate violence of evil passions, that they never suffer their subjects to act with consistency, but, torn by conflicting energies, the gratification of one propensity is destruction to the enjoyment of another; and the moment in which they imagine happiness in their grasp, is to them the moment of disappointment. Thus it was with the Baron; his soul seemed to attain its full enjoyment in the contemplation of revenge, till the idea of Mary inflamed his heart with an opposite passion; his wishes had caught new ardor from disappointment, for he had heard that Mary had been once in the power of his emissaries; and perhaps the pain which recoils upon the mind from every fruitless effort of wickedness, served to encrease the energies of his desires. He spurned the thought of relinquishing the pursuit, yet there appeared to be no method of obtaining its object, but by sacrificing his favourite passion; for he had little doubt of obtaining Mary, when it should be known that he resolved not to grant the life of the Earl upon any other ransom. The balance of these passions hung in his mind in such nice equilibrium, that it was for some time uncertain which would preponderate; revenge, at length, yielded to love; but he resolved to preserve the torture of expected death, by keeping the Earl ignorant of his reprieve till the last moment.

The Earl awaited death with the same stern fortitude with which he received its sentence, and was led from the tower to the platform of the castle, silent and unmoved. He beheld the preparations for his execution, the instruments of death, the guards arranged in files, with an undaunted mind. The glare of externals had no longer power over his imagination. He beheld every object with indifference, but that on which his eye now rested; it was on the murderer, who exhibited himself in all the pride of exulting conquest: he started at the sight, and his soul shrunk back upon itself. Disdaining, however, to appear disconcerted, he endeavoured to resume his dignity, when the remembrance of his mother, overwhelmed with sorrow, rushed upon his mind, and quite unmanned him; the tears started in his eyes, and he sunk senseless on the ground.

On recovering, he found himself in his prison, and he was informed that the Baron had granted him a respite. Malcolm mistaking the cause of disorder in the Earl, thought he had stretched his sufferings to their utmost limits; he therefore had ordered him to be re-conveyed to the tower.

A scene so striking and so public as that which had just been performed at the castle of Dunbayne, was a subject of discourse to the whole country; it was soon reported to the Countess with a variety of additional circumstances, among which it was affirmed, that the Earl had been really executed. Overwhelmed with this intelligence, Matilda relapsed into her former disorder. Sickness had rendered Mary less able to support the shock, and to apply that comfort to the afflictions of her mother, which had once been so successfully administered. The physician pronounced the malady of the Countess to be seated in the mind, and beyond the reach of human skill, when one day a letter was brought to her, the superscription of which was written in the hand of Osbert; she knew the characters, and bursting the seal, read that her son was yet alive, and did not despair of throwing himself once more at her feet. He requested that the remains of his clan might immediately attempt his release. He described in what part of the castle his prison was situated, and thought, that by the assistance of long scaling-ladders and ropes, contrived in the manner he directed, he might be able to effect his escape through the grate. This letter was a reviving cordial to the Countess and to Mary.

Alleyn was indefatigable in collecting followers for the enterprize he had engaged in. On receiving intelligence of the safety of the Earl, he visited the clan, and was strenuous in exhorting them to immediate action. They required little incitement to a cause in which every heart was so much interested, and for which every hand was already busied in preparation. These preparations were at length completed; Alleyn, at the head of his party, joined the assembled clan. The Countess for a second time beheld from the ramparts the departure of her people upon the same hazardous enterprize; the present scene revived in her mind a sad remembrance of the past: the same tender fears, and the same prayers for success she now gave to their departure; and when they faded in distance from her sight, she returned into the castle dissolved in tears. The heart of Mary was torn by a complex sorrow, and incapable of longer concealing from herself the interest she took in the departure of Alleyn, her agitation became more apparent. The Countess in vain endeavoured to compose her mind. Mary, affected by her tender concern, and prompted by the natural ingenuousness of her disposition, longed to make her the confidant of her weakness, if weakness that can be termed which arises from gratitude, and from the admiration of great and generous qualities; but delicacy and timidity arrested the half-formed sentence, and closed her lips in silence. Her health gradually declined under the secret agitation of her mind; her physician knew her disorder to originate in suppressed sorrow, and advised, as the best cordial, a confidential friend. Matilda now perceived the cause of her grief; her former passing observations recurred to her memory, and justified her discernment. She strove by every soothing effort to win her to her confidence. Mary, oppressed by the idea of ungenerous concealment, resolved at length to unveil her heart to a mother so tender of her happiness. She told her all her sentiments. The Countess suffered a distress almost equal to that of her daughter; her affectionate heart swelled with equal wishes for her happiness; she admired with warmest gratitude the noble and aspiring virtues of the young Highlander; but the proud nobility of her soul repelled with quick vivacity every idea of union with a youth of such ignoble birth: she regarded the present attachment as the passing impression of youthful fancy, and believed that gentle reasoning, aided by time and endeavour, would conquer the enthusiasm of love. Mary listened with attention to the reasonings of the Countess; her judgment acknowledged their justness, while her heart regretted their force. She resolved, however, to overcome an attachment which would produce so much distress to her family and to herself. Notwithstanding her endeavours to exclude Alleyn from her thoughts, the generous and heroic qualities of his mind burst upon her memory in all their splendor, she could not but be conscious that he loved her; she saw the struggles of his soul, and the delicacy of his passion, which made him ever retire in the most profound and respectful silence from its object. She solicited her mother to assist in expelling the destructive image from her mind. The Countess exerted every effort to amuse her to forgetfulness; every hour, except those which were given to exercises necessary for her health, was devoted to the cultivation of her mind, and the improvement of her various accomplishments. These endeavours were not unsuccessful; the Countess with joy observed the returning health and tranquillity of her daughter; and Mary almost believed she had taught herself to forget. These engagements served also to beguile the tedious moments which must intervene, ere news could arrive from Alleyn concerning the probable success of the enterprize.

Misery yet dwelt in the castle of Dunbayne; for there the virtues were captive, while the vices reigned despotic. The mind of the Baron, ardent and restless, knew no peace: torn by conflicting passions, he was himself the victim of their power.

The Earl knew that his life hung upon the caprice of a tyrant; his mind was nerved for the worst; yet the letter which the compassion of one of his guards, at the risque of his life, had undertaken to convey to the Countess, afforded him a faint hope that his people might yet effect his escape. In this expectation, he spent hour after hour at his grate, wishing, with trembling anxiety, to behold his clan advancing over the distant hills. These hills became at length, in a situation so barren of real comforts, a source of ideal pleasure to him. He was always at the grate, and often, in the fine evenings of summer saw the ladies, whose appearance had so strongly excited his admiration* and pity, walk on a terrace below the tower. One very fine evening, under the pleasing impressions of hope for himself, and compassion for them, his sufferings for a time lost their acuteness. He longed to awaken their sympathy, and make known to them that they had a fellow-prisoner. The parting sun trembled on the tops of the mountains, and a softer shade fell upon the distant landscape. The sweet tranquillity of evening threw an air of tender melancholy over his mind: his sorrows for a while were hushed; and under the enthusiasm of the hour, he composed the following stanzas, which, having committed them to paper, he the next evening dropp'd upon the terrace.

SONNET*

Hail! to the hallow'd hill, the circling lawn,
　The breezy upland, and the mountain stream!
The last tall pine that earliest meets the dawn,
　And glistens latest to the western gleam!

Hail! every distant hill, and downland plain!
　Your dew-hid beauties Fancy oft unveils;
What time to shepherd's reed, or poet's strain,
　Sorrowing my heart its destin'd woe bewails.

Blest are the fairy hour, the twilight shade
　Of Ev'ning, wand'ring thro' her woodlands dear,
Sweet the still sound that steals along the glade;
　'Tis fancy wafts it, and her vot'ries hear.

'Tis fancy wafts it!—and how sweet the sound!
　I hear it now the distant hills uplong;
While fairy echos from their dells around,
　And woods, and wilds, the feeble notes prolong!

He had the pleasure to observe that the paper was taken up by the ladies, who immediately retired into the castle.

CHAPTER V

ONE morning early, the Earl discerned a martial band emerging from the verge of the horizon; his heart welcomed his hopes, which were soon confirmed into certainty. It was his faithful people, led on by Alleyn. It was their design to surround and attack the castle; and though their numbers gave them but little hopes of conquest, they yet believed that, in the tumult of the engagement, they might procure the deliverance of the Earl. With this view they advanced to the walls. The centinels had descried them at a distance; the alarm was given; the trumpets sounded, and the walls of the castle were filled with men. The Baron was present, and directed the preparations. The secret purpose of his soul was fixed. The clan surrounded the fosse, into which they threw bundles of faggots, and gave the signal of attack. Scaling ladders were thrown up to the window of the tower. The Earl, invigorated with hope and joy, had by the force of his arm, almost wrenched from its fastening, one of the iron bars of the grate; his foot was lifted to the stanchion,* ready to aid him in escaping through the opening, when he was seized by the guards of the Baron, and conveyed precipitately from the prison. He was led, indignant and desperate, to the lofty ramparts of the castle, from whence he beheld Alleyn and his clan, whose eager eyes were once more blessed with the sight of their Chief;—they were blessed but for a moment; they beheld their Lord in chains, surrounded with guards, and with the instruments of death. Animated, however, with a last hope, they renewed the attack with redoubled fury, when the trumpets of the Baron sounded a parley,* and they suspended their arms. The Baron appeared on the ramparts; Alleyn advanced to hear him. 'The moment of attack,' cried the Baron, 'is the moment of death to your Chief. If you wish to preserve his life, desist from the assault, and depart in peace; and bear this message to the Countess your mistress:—the Baron Malcolm will accept no other ransom for the life and the liberty of the Earl, than her beauteous daughter, whom he now sues to become his wife. If she accedes to these terms, the Earl is instantly liberated,—if she refuses, he dies.'* The emotions of the Earl, and of Alleyn, on hearing these words, were inexpressible. The Earl spurned, with haughty virtue, the base concession. 'Give me death,' cried he with loud impatience; 'the house of Athlin shall not be dishonoured by alliance with a murderer: renew the attack, my brave people; since you cannot save the life, revenge the death of your Chief; he dies contented, since his death preserves his family from dishonour.' The guards instantly surrounded the Earl.

Alleyn, whose heart, torn by contending emotions, was yet true to the impulse of honour, on observing this, instantly threw down his arms, refusing to obey the commands of the Earl; a hostage for whose life he demanded, while he hastened to the castle of Athlin with the conditions of the Baron. The clan, following the example of Alleyn, rested on their arms, while a few prepared to depart with him on the embassy. In vain were the remonstrances and the commands of the Earl; his people loved him too well to obey them, and his heart was filled with anguish when he saw Alleyn depart from the walls.

The situation of Alleyn was highly pitiable; all the firm virtues of his soul were called upon to support it. He was commissioned on an embassy, the alternate conditions of which would bring misery on the woman he adored, or death to the friend whom he loved.

When the arrival of Alleyn was announced to the Countess, impatient joy thrilled in her bosom; for she had no doubt that he brought offers of accommodation; and no ransom was presented to her imagination, which she would not willingly give for the restoration of her son. At the sound of Alleyn's voice, those tumults which had began to subside in the heart of Mary, were again revived, and she awoke to the mournful certainty of hopeless endeavour. Yet she could not repress a strong emotion of joy on again beholding him. The soft blush of her cheek shewed the colours of her mind, while, in endeavouring to shade her feelings, she impelled them into stronger light.

The agitations of Alleyn almost subdued his strength, when he entered the presence of the Countess; and his visage, on which was impressed deep distress, and the paleness of fear, betrayed the inward workings of his soul. Matilda was instantly seized with apprehension for the safety of her son, and in a tremulous voice, enquired his fate. Alleyn told her he was well, proceeding with tender caution to acquaint her with the business of his embassy, and with the scene to which he had lately been witness. The sentence of the Baron fell like the stroke of death upon the heart of Mary, who fainted at the words. Alleyn flew to support her. In endeavouring to revive her daughter, the Countess was diverted for a time from the anguish which this intelligence must naturally impart. It was long ere Mary returned to life, and she returned only to a sense of wretchedness. The critical situation of Matilda can scarcely be felt in its full extent. Torn by the conflict of opposite interests, her brain was the seat of tumult, and wild dismay. Which ever way she looked, destruction closed the view. The murderer of the husband, now sought to murder the happiness of the daughter. On the sentence of the mother hung the final fate of the son. In rejecting these terms, she would give him instant death; in accepting them, her conduct would be repugnant to the feelings of indignant virtue, and to the tender injured memory of her murdered Lord. She would destroy for ever the peace of her daughter, and the honour of her house. To effect his deliverance by force of arms was utterly impracticable, since the Baron had declared, that 'the moment of attack should be the moment of death to the Earl.' Honour, humanity, parental tenderness, bade her save her son; yet, by a strange contrariety of interests, the same virtues pleaded with a voice equally powerful, for the reverse of the sentence. Hitherto hope had still illumined her mind with a distant ray; she now found herself suddenly involved in the darkness of despair, whose glooms were interrupted only by the gleams of horror which arose from the altar, on which was to be sacrificed one of her beloved children. Her mind shrunk from the idea of uniting her daughter to the murderer of her father. The ferocious character of Malcolm was alone sufficient to blight for ever the happiness of the woman whose fate should be connected with his. To give to the murderer the child of the murdered was a thought too horrid to rest upon. The Countess rejected with force the Baron's offer of exchange, when the bleeding figure of her beloved son, pale and convulsed in death, started on her imagination, and stretched her brain almost to frenzy.

Meanwhile Mary suffered a conflict equally dreadful. Nature had bestowed on her a heart susceptible of all the fine emotions of delicate passion; a heart which vibrated in unison with the sweetest feelings of humanity; a mind, quick in perceiving the nicest lines of moral rectitude, and strenuous in endeavouring to act up to its perceptions. These gifts were unnecessary to make her sensible of the wretchedness of her present situation; of which a common mind would have felt the misery; they served, however, to sharpen the points of affliction, to encrease their force, and to disclose, in stronger light, the various horrors of her situation. Fraternal love and pity called loudly upon her to resign herself into the power of the man whom, from the earliest dawn of perception, she had contemplated with trembling aversion and horror. The memory of her murdered parent, every feeling dear to virtue, the tremulous, but forceful voice of love awakened her heart, and each opposed, with wild impetuosity, every other sentiment. Her soul shrunk back with terror from the idea of union with the Baron. Could she bear to receive, in marriage, that hand which was stained with the blood of her father?—The polluted touch would freeze her heart in horror!—could she bear to pass her life with the man, who had for ever blasted the smiling days of him who gave her being?—With the man who would stand before her eyes a perpetual monument of misery to herself, and of dishonour to her family? whose chilling aspect would repel every amiable and generous affection, and strike them back upon her heart only to wound it? To cherish the love of the noble virtues, would be to cherish the remembrance of her dead father, and of her living lover. How wretched must be her situation, when to obliterate from her memory the image of virtue, could alone afford her a chance of obtaining a horrid tranquillity; virtue which is so dear to the human heart, that when her form forsakes us, we pursue her shadow. Wherever in search of comfort she directed her aching sight, Misery's haggard countenance obtruded on her view. Here she beheld herself entombed in the arms of the murderer;—there, the spectacle of her beloved brother, encircled with chains, and awaiting the stroke of death, arose to her imagination; the scene was too affecting; fancy gave her the horrors of reality. The reflection, that through her he suffered, that she yet might save him from destruction, broke with irresistible force upon her mind, and instantly bore away every opposing feeling.—She resolved, that since she must be wretched, she would be nobly wretched; since misery demanded one sacrifice, she would devote herself the victim.

With these thoughts, she entered the apartment of the Countess, whose concurrence was necessary to ratify her resolves, and, having declared them, awaited in trembling expectation her decision. Matilda had suffered a distraction of mind, which the nature of no former trial had occasioned her. On the unfortunate death of a husband tenderly beloved, she had suffered all the sorrow which tenderness, and all the shock which the manner of his death could occasion. The event, however, shocking as it was, did not hang upon circumstances over which she had an influence; it was decided by an higher power;—it was decided, and never could be recalled; she had there no dreadful choice of horrors, no evil ratified by her own voice, to taint with deadly recollections her declining days. This choice, though forced upon her by the power of a tyrant, she would still consider as in part her own; and the thought that she was compelled to doom to destruction one of her children, harrowed up her soul almost to frenzy.

Her mind, at length exhausted with excess of feeling, was now fallen into a state of cold and silent despair; she became insensible to the objects around her, almost to the sense of her own sufferings, and the voice, and the proposal of her daughter, scarcely awakened her powers of perception. 'He shall live,' said Mary, in a voice broken and tender; 'He shall live, I am ready to become the sacrifice.' Tears prevented her proceeding. At the word 'live,' the Countess raised her eyes, and threw round her a look of wildness, which settling on the features of Mary, softened into an expression of ineffable tenderness, she waved her head, and turned to the window. A few tears bedewed her cheek; they fell like the drops of Heaven upon the withered plant, reviving and expanding its dying foliage;* they were the first her eyes had known since the fatal news had reached her. Recovering herself a little, she sent for Alleyn, who was still in the castle. She wished to consult with him, whether there was not yet a possibility of effecting the escape of the Earl. In afflictions of whatever degree, where death has not already fixed the events in certainty, the mind shoots almost beyond the sphere of possibility in search of hope, and seldom relinquishes the fond illusion, till the stroke of reality dissolves the enchantment. Thus it was with Matilda; after the grief produced by the first stroke of this disaster was somewhat abated, she was inclined to think that her situation might not prove so desperate as she imagined; and her heart was warmed by a remote hope, that there might yet be devised some method of procuring the escape of the Earl. Alleyn came; he came in the trembling expectation of receiving the decision of the Countess, and in the intention of offering to engage in any enterprize, however hazardous, for the enlargement of the Earl. He repelled, with instant force, every idea of Mary's becoming the wife of Malcolm; the thought was too full of agony to be endured, and he threw the sensation from his heart as a poison which would destroy the pulse of life. To preserve Mary from a misery so exquisite, and to save the life of the Earl, he was willing to encounter any hazard; to meet death itself as an evil which appeared less dreadful than either of the former. He came prepared with this resolution, and it served to support that fortitude which affliction had disturbed, though it could not subdue. When he came again to the Countess, his distress was heightened by the scene before him; he beheld her leaning on a sofa,* pale and silent; her unconscious eyes were fixed on an opposite window; her countenance was touched with a wildness expressive of the disorder of her mind, and she remained for some time insensible of his approach. Such is the fluctuation of a mind overcome by distress, that if for a moment a ray of hope chears* its darkness, it vanishes at the touch of recollection. Mary was standing near the Countess, whose hand she held to her bosom. Her present sorrow had heightened the natural pensiveness of her countenance, and shaded her features with an interesting langour, more enchanting than the vivacity of blooming health; her eyes sought to avoid Alleyn, as an object dangerous to the resolution she had formed. Matilda remained absorbed in thought. Mary wished to repeat the purpose of her soul, but her voice trembled, and the half-formed sentence died away on her lips. Alleyn enquired the commands of the Countess. 'I am ready,' said Mary, at length, in a low and tremulous voice, 'to give myself the victim to the Baron's revenge.—I will save my brother.' At these words, the heart of Alleyn grew cold. Mary, overcome by the effort which they had occasioned her, scarcely finished the sentence; her nerves shook, a mist fell over her eyes, and she sunk on the sofa by which she had stood. Alleyn hung over the couch in silent agony, watching her return to life. By the assistance of those about her, she soon revived. Alleyn, in the joy which he felt at her recovery, forgot for a moment his situation, and pressed with ardor her hand to his bosom. Mary, whose senses were yet scarcely recollected, yielded unconsciously to the softness of her heart, and betrayed its situation by a smile so tender, as to thrill the breast of Alleyn with the sweet certainty of being loved. Hitherto his passion had been chilled by the despair which the vast superiority of her birth occasioned, and by the modesty which forbade him to imagine that he had merit sufficient to arrest the eye of the accomplished Mary. Perhaps, too, the diffidence natural to genuine love, might contribute to deceive him. It was not till this moment, that he experienced that certainty which awakened in his heart a sense of delight hitherto unknown to him. For a moment he forgot the distresses of the castle, and his own situation; every idea faded from his mind, but the one he had so lately acquired; and in that moment he seemed to taste perfect felicity. Recollection, however, with all its train of black dependancies soon returned, and plunged him in a misery as poignant as the joy from which he was now precipitated.

The Countess was now sufficiently composed to enter on the subject nearest her heart. Alleyn caught, with eagerness, her mention of attempting the deliverance of the Earl, for the possibility of accomplishing which, he declared himself willing to encounter any danger: he seconded so warmly the design, and spoke with such flattering probability of success, that the spirits of Matilda began once more to revive; yet she trembled to encourage hopes which hung on such perilous uncertainty. It was agreed, that Alleyn should consult with the most able and trusty of the clan, whom age or infirmity had detained from battle, on the means most likely to ensure success, and then proceed immediately on the expedition: having first delivered to the Baron a message from the Countess, requiring time for deliberation upon a choice so important, and importing that an answer should be returned at the expiration of a fortnight.

Alleyn accordingly assembled those whom he judged most worthy of the council: various schemes were proposed, none of which appeared likely to succeed; when it was recollected that the Earl might possibly have been removed from the tower to some new place of confinement, which it would be necessary first to discover, that the plan might be adapted to the situation. It was therefore concluded to suspend further consultation till Alleyn had obtained the requisite information; and that in the mean time he should deliver to Malcolm the message of the Countess: for these purposes Alleyn immediately set out for the castle.

CHAPTER VI

THE castle of Dunbayne was still the scene of triumph, and of wretchedness. Malcolm, exulting in his scheme, already beheld Mary at his feet, and the Earl retiring in an anguish more poignant than that of death. He was surprized that his invention had not before supplied him with this means of torture: for the first time he welcomed love, as the instrument of his revenge; and the charms of Mary were heightened to his imagination by the ardent colours of this passion. He was confirmed in his resolves, never to relinquish the Earl, but on the conditions he had offered; and thus for ever would he preserve the house of Athlin a monument of his triumph.

Osbert, for greater security, was conveyed from the tower into a more centrical* part of the castle, to an apartment spacious but gloomy, whose gothic windows partly excluding light, threw a solemnity around, which chilled the heart almost to horror. He heeded not this; his heart was occupied with horrors of its own. He was now involved in a misery more intricate, and more dreadful, than his imagination had yet painted. To die, was to him, who had so long contemplated the near approach of death, a familiar and transient evil; but to see, even in idea, his family involved in infamy, and in union with the murderer, was the stroke which pierced his heart to its center. He feared that the cruel tenderness of the mother would tempt Matilda to accept the offers of the Baron; and he scarcely doubted, that the noble Mary would resign herself the price of his life. He would have written to the Countess to have forbidden her acceptance of the terms, and to have declared his fixed resolution to die, but that he had no means of conveying to her a letter; the soldier who had so generously undertaken the conveyance of his former one, having soon after disappeared from his station. The manly fortitude which had supported him through his former trials, did not desert him in this hour of darkness; habituated so long to struggle with opposing feelings, he had acquired the art of managing them; his mind attained a confidence in its powers;

resistance served only to increase its strength, and to confirm the magnanimity of its nature.

Alleyn had now joined the clan, and was ardent in pursuit of the necessary intelligence. He learned that the Earl had been removed from the tower, but in what part of the castle he was now confined he could not discover; on this point all was vague conjecture. That he was alive, was only judged from the policy of the Baron, whose ardent passion for Mary was now well understood. Alleyn employed every stratagem his invention could suggest, to discover the prison of the Earl, but without success: at length compelled to deliver to Malcolm the message of the Countess, he demanded as a preliminary, that the Earl should be shewn to his people from the ramparts, that they might be certain he was still alive. Alleyn hoped that his appearance would lead to a discovery of the place of his imprisonment, purposing to observe narrowly the way by which he should retire.

The Earl appeared in safety on the ramparts, amid the shouts and acclamations of his people; the Baron frowning defiance, was seen at his side. Alleyn advanced to the walls, and delivered the message of Matilda. Osbert started at its purpose; he foresaw that deliberation portended compliance:—stung with the thought, he swore aloud he never would survive the infamy of the concession; and addressing himself to Alleyn, commanded him instantly to return to the Countess, and bid her spurn the base compliance, as she feared to sacrifice both her children to the murderer of their father. At these words, a smile of haughty triumph marked the features of the Baron, and he turned from Osbert in silent joy and exultation. The Earl was led off by the guards. Alleyn endeavoured in vain to mark the way they took; the lofty walls soon concealed them from his view.

Alleyn now experienced how strenuously a vigorous mind protects its favourite hope; wayward circumstances may shock, disappointment may check it; but it rises superior to opposition and traverses the sphere of possibility to accomplish its purpose. Alleyn did not yet despair, but he was perplexed in what manner to proceed.

In his way from the ramparts, Osbert was surprised by the appearance of two ladies at a window near which he passed: the agitation of his mind did not prevent his recognizing them as the same he had observed from the grates of the tower, with such lively admiration, and who had excited in his mind so much pity and curiosity. In the midst of his distress, his thoughts had often dwelt on the sweet graces of the younger, and he had sighed to obtain the story of her sorrows; for the melancholy which hung upon her features proclaimed her to be unfortunate. They now stood observing Osbert as he passed, and their eyes expressed the pity which his situation inspired. He gazed earnestly and mournfully upon them, and when he entered his prison, again enquired concerning them, but the same inflexible silence was preserved on the subject.

As the Earl sat one day musing in his prison, his eyes involuntarily fixed upon a pannel* in the opposite wainscot;—he observed that it was differently formed from the rest, and that its projection was somewhat greater; a hope started into his mind, and he quitted his seat to examine it. He perceived that it was surrounded by a small crack, and on pushing it with his hands it shook under them. Certain that it was something more than a pannel, he exerted all his strength against it, but without producing any new effect. Having tried various means to move it without success, he gave up the experiment, and returned to his seat melancholy and disappointed. Several days passed without any further notice being taken of the wainscot; unwilling, however, to relinquish a last hope, he returned to the examination, when, in endeavouring to remove the pannel, his foot accidentally hit against one corner, and it suddenly flew open. It had been contrived that a spring which was concealed within, and which fastened the partition, should receive its impulse from the pressure of a certain part of the pannel, which was now touched by the foot of the Earl. His joy on the discovery cannot be expressed. An apartment wide and forlorn, like that which formed his prison, now lay before him; the windows, which were high and arched, were decorated with painted glass; the floor was paved with marble; and it seemed to be the deserted remains of a place of worship. Osbert traversed, with hesitating steps, its dreary length, towards a pair of folding doors, large and of oak, which closed the apartment: these he opened; a gallery, gloomy and vast, appeared beyond; the windows, which were in the same style of Gothic architecture with the former, were shaded by thick ivy that almost excluded the light. Osbert stood at the entrance uncertain whether to proceed; he listened, but heard no footstep in his prison, and determined to go on. The gallery terminated on the left in a large winding stair-case, old and apparently neglected, which led to a hall below; on the right was a door, low, and rather obscure. Osbert, apprehensive of discovery, passed the staircase, and opened the door, when a suite of noble apartments, magnificently furnished, was disclosed to his wondering eyes. He proceeded onward without perceiving any person, but having passed the second room, heard the faint sobs of a person weeping; he stood for a moment, undetermined whether to proceed; but an irresistible curiosity impelled him forward, and he entered an apartment, in which were seated the beautiful strangers, whose appearance had so much interested his feelings. The elder of the ladies was dissolved in tears and a casket and some papers lay open on a table beside her. The younger was so intent upon a drawing, which she seemed to be finishing, as not to observe the entrance of the Earl; the elder lady, on perceiving him, arose in some confusion, and the surprize in her eyes seemed to demand an explanation of so unaccountable a visit. The Earl, surprised at what he beheld, stepped back with an intention of retiring; but recollecting that the intrusion demanded an apology, he returned. The grace with which he excused himself, confirmed the impression which his figure had already made on the mind of Laura, which was the name of the younger lady; who on looking up, discovered a countenance in which dignity and sweetness were happily blended. She appeared to be about twenty, her person was of the middle stature, extremely delicate, and very elegantly formed. The bloom of her youth was shaded by a soft and pensive melancholy, which communicated an expression to her fine blue eyes, extremely interesting. Her features were partly concealed by the beautiful luxuriance of her auburn hair, which curling round her face, descended in tresses on her bosom; every feminine grace played around her; and the simple dignity of her air declared the purity and the nobility of her mind. On perceiving the Earl, a faint blush animated her cheek, and she involuntarily quitted the drawing upon which she had been engaged.

If the former imperfect view he had caught of Laura had given an impression to the heart of Osbert, it now received a stronger character from the opportunity afforded him of contemplating her beauty. He concluded that the Baron, attracted by her charms, had entrapped her into his power, and detained her in the castle an unwilling prisoner. In this conjecture he was confirmed by the mournful cast of her countenance, and by the mystery which appeared to surround her. Fired by this idea, he melted in compassion for her sufferings; which compassion was tinctured and increased by the passion which now glowed in his heart. At that moment he forgot the danger of his present situation; he forgot even that he was a prisoner; and awake only to the wish of alleviating her sorrows, he rejected cold and useless delicacy, and resolved, if possible, to learn the cause of her misfortunes. Addressing himself to the Baroness, 'if, Madam,' said he, 'I could by any means soften the affliction which I cannot affect not to perceive, and which has so warmly interested my feelings, I should regard this as one of the most happy moments of my life; a life marked alas! too strongly with misery! but misery has not been useless, since it has taught me sympathy.' The Baroness was no stranger to the character and the misfortunes of the Earl. Herself the victim of oppression, she knew how to commiserate the sufferings of others. She had ever felt a tender compassion for the misfortunes of Osbert, and did not now with-hold sincere expressions of sympathy, and of gratitude, for the interest which he felt in her sorrow. She expressed her surprize at seeing him thus at liberty; but observing the chains which encircled his hands, she shuddered, and guessed a part of the truth. He explained to her the discovery of the pannel, by which circumstance he had found his way into that apartment. The idea of aiding him to escape, rushed upon the mind of the Baroness, but was repressed by the consideration of her own confined situation; and she was compelled, with mournful reluctance, to resign that thought which reverence for the character of the late Earl, and compassion for the misfortunes of the present, had inspired. She lamented her inability to assist him, and informed him that herself and her daughter were alike prisoners with himself; that the walls of the castle were the limits of their liberty; and that they had suffered the pressure of tyranny for fifteen years. The Earl expressed the indignation which he felt at this recital, and solicited the Baroness to confide in his integrity; and, if the relation would not be too painful to her, to honour him so far as to acquaint him by what cruel means she fell into the power of Malcolm. The Baroness, apprehensive for his safety reminded him of the risk of discovery by a longer absence from his prison; and, thanking him again for the interest he took in her sufferings, assured him of her warmest wishes for his deliverance, and that if an opportunity ever offered, she would acquaint him with the sad particulars of her story. The eyes of Osbert made known that gratitude which it was difficult for his tongue to utter. Tremulously he solicited the consolation of sometimes revisiting the apartments of the Baroness; a permission which would give him some intervals of comfort amid the many hours of torment to which he was condemned. The Baroness, in compassion to his sufferings, granted the request. The Earl departed, gazing on Laura with eyes of mournful tenderness; yet he was pleased with what had passed, and retired to his prison in one of those peaceful intervals which are known even to the wretched. He found all quiet, and closing the pannel in safety, sat down to consider the past, and anticipate the future. He was flattered with hopes, that the discovery of the pannel might aid him to escape; the glooms of despondence which had lately enveloped his mind, gradually disappeared, and joy once more illumined his prospects; but it was the sunshine of an April morn, deceitful and momentary. He recollected that the castle was beset with guards, whose vigilance was insured by the severity of the Baron; he remembered that the strangers, who had taken so kind an interest in his fate, were prisoners like himself; and that he had no generous soldier to teach him the secret windings of the castle, and to accompany him in flight. His imagination was haunted by the image of Laura; vainly he strove to disguise from himself the truth; his heart constantly belied the sophistry of his reasonings. Unwarily he had drank the draught of love, and he was compelled to acknowledge the fatal indiscretion. He could not, however, resolve to throw from his heart the delicious poison; he could not resolve to see her no more.

The painful apprehension for his safety, which his forbearing to renew the visit he had so earnestly solicited, would occasion the Baroness; the apparent disrespect it would convey; the ardent curiosity with which be longed to obtain the history of her misfortunes; the lively interest he felt in learning the situation of Laura, with respect to the Baron; and the hope,—the wild hope, with which he deluded his reason, that he might be able to assist them, determined him to repeat the visit. Under these illusions, the motive which principally impelled him to the interview was concealed.

In the mean time Alleyn had returned to the castle of Athlin with the resolutions of the Earl; whose resolves served only to aggravate the distress of its fair inhabitants. Alleyn, however, unwilling to crush a last hope, tenderly concealed from them the circumstance of the Earl's removal from the tower: silently and almost hopelessly meditating to discover his prison; and administered that comfort to the Countess, and to Mary, which his own expectation would not suffer him to participate. He retired in haste to the veterans whom he had before assembled, and acquainted them with the removal of the Earl; which circumstance must for the present suspend their consultations. He left them, therefore, and instantly returned to the clan: there to prosecute his enquiries. Every possible exertion was made to obtain the necessary intelligence, but without success. The moment in which the Baron would demand the answer of the Countess, was now fast approaching, and every heart sunk in despair, when one night the centinels of the camp were alarmed by the approach of men, who hailed them in unknown voices; fearful of surprize, they surrounded the strangers, and led them to Alleyn; to whom they related, that they fled from the capricious tyranny of Malcolm, and sought refuge in the camp of his enemy; whose misfortunes they bewailed, and in whose cause they enlisted. Rejoiced at the circumstance, yet doubtful of its truth, Alleyn interrogated the soldiers concerning the prison of the Earl. From them he learned, that Osbert was confined in a part of the castle extremely difficult of access; and that any plan of escape must be utterly impracticable without the assistance of one well acquainted with the various intricacies of the pile. An opportunity of success was now presented, with which the most sanguine hopes of Alleyn had never flattered him. He received from the soldiers strong assurances of assistance; from them, likewise, he learned, that discontent reigned, among the people of the Baron; who, impatient of the yoke of tyranny, only waited a favourable opportunity to throw it off, and resume the rights of nature.* That the vigilant suspicions of Malcolm excited him to punish with the harshest severity every appearance of inattention; that being condemned to suffer a very heavy punishment for a slight offence, they had eluded the impending misery, and the future oppression of their Chief, by desertion.

Alleyn immediately convened a council, before whom the soldiers were brought; they repeated their former assertions; and one of the fugitives added, that he had a brother, whose place of guard over the person of the Earl on that night, had made it difficult to elude observation, and had prevented his escaping with them; that on the night of the morrow he stood guard at the gate of the lesser draw-bridge, where the centinels were few; that he was himself willing to risque the danger of conversing with him; and had little doubt of gaining him to assist in the deliverance of the Earl. At these words, the heart of Alleyn throbbed with joy. He promised large rewards to the brave soldier and to his brother, if they undertook the enterprize. His companion was well acquainted with the subterraneous passages of the rock, and expressed himself desirous of being useful. The hopes of Alleyn every instant grew stronger; and he vainly wished, at that moment, to communicate to the Earl's unhappy family the joy which dilated his heart.

The eve of the following day was fixed upon to commence their designs; when James should endeavour to gain his brother to their purpose. Having adjusted these matters, they retired to rest for the remainder of the night; but sleep had fled the eyes of Alleyn; anxious expectation filled his mind; and he saw, in the waking visions of fancy, the meeting of the Earl with his family: he anticipated the thanks he should receive from the lovely

Mary; and sighed at the recollection, that thanks were all for which he could ever dare to hope.

At length the dawn appeared, and waked the clan to hopes and prospects far different from those of the preceding morn. The hours hung heavily on the expectation of Alleyn, whose mind was filled with solicitude for the event of the meeting between the brothers. Night at length came to his wishes. The darkness was interrupted only by the faint light of the moon moving through the watery and broken clouds, which enveloped the horizon. Tumultuous gusts of wind broke at intervals the silence of the hour. Alleyn watched the movements of the castle; he observed the lights successively disappear. The bell from the watch-tower chimed one; all was still within the walls; and James ventured forth to the draw-bridge. The draw-bridge divided in the center, and the half next the plains was down; he mounted it, and in a low yet firm voice called on Edmund. No answer was returned; and he began to fear that his brother had already quitted the castle. He remained some time in silent suspense before he repeated the call, when he heard the gate of the draw-bridge gently unbarred, and Edmund appeared. He was surprized to see James, and bade him instantly fly the danger that surrounded him. The Baron, incensed at the frequent desertion of his soldiers, had sent out people in pursuit, and had promised considerable rewards for the apprehension of the fugitives. James, undaunted by what he heard, kept his ground, resolved to urge his purpose to the point. Happily the centinels who stood guard with Edmund, overcome with the effect of a potion he had administered to favour his escape, were sunk in sleep, and the soldiers conducted their discourse in a low voice without interruption.

Edmund was unwilling   defer his flight, and possessed not resolution sufficient to encounter the hazard of the enterprize, till the proffered reward consoled his self-denial, and roused his slumbering courage. He was well acquainted with the sub-terraneous avenues of the castle; the only remaining difficulty, was that of deceiving the vigilance of his fellow-centinels, whose watchfulness made it impossible for the Earl to quit his prison unperceived. The soldiers who were to mount guard with him on the following night, were stationed in a distant part of the castle, till the hour of their removal to the door of the prison; it was, therefore, difficult to administer to them that draught which had steeped in forgetfulness the senses of his present associates. To confide to their integrity, and endeavour to win them to his purpose, was certainly to give his life into their hands, and probably to aggravate the disastrous fate of the Earl. This scheme was beset too thick with dangers to be hazarded, and their invention could furnish them with none more promising. It was, however, agreed, that on the following night, Edmund should seize the moment of opportunity to impart to the Earl the designs of his friends, and to consult on the means of accomplishing them. Thus concluding, James returned in safety to the tent of Alleyn, where the most considerable of the clan were assembled, there awaiting with impatient solicitude, his arrival. The hopes of Alleyn were somewhat chilled by the report of the soldier; from the vigilance which beset the doors of the prison, escape from thence appeared impracticable. He was condemned, however, to linger in suspense till the third night from the present, when the return of Edmund to his station at the bridge would enable him again to commune with his brother. But Alleyn was unsuspicious of a circumstance which would utterly have defeated his hopes, and whose consequence threatened destruction to all their schemes. A centinel on duty upon that part of the rampart which surmounted the draw-bridge, had been alarmed by hearing the gate unbar, and approaching the wall, had perceived a man standing on the half of the bridge which was dropped, and in converse with some person on the castle walls. He drew as near as the wall would permit, and endeavoured to listen to their discourse. The gloom of night prevented his recognizing the person on the bridge; but he could clearly distinguish the voice of Edmund in that of the man who was addressed. Excited by new wonder, he gave all his attention to discover the subject of their conversation. The distance occasioned between the brothers by the suspended half of the bridge, obliged them to speak in a somewhat higher tone than they would otherwise have done; and the centinel gathered sufficient from their discourse, to learn that they were concerting the rescue of the Earl; that the night of Edmund's watch at the prison was to be the night of enterprize; and that some friends of the Earl were to await him in the environs of the castle. All this he carefully treasured up, and the next morning communicated it to his comrades.

On the following evening the Earl, yielding to the impulse of his heart, once more unclosed his partition, and sought the apartments of the Baroness. She received him with expressions of satisfaction; while the artless pleasure which lighted up the countenance of Laura, awakened the pulse of rapture in that heart which had long throbbed only to misery. The Earl reminded the Baroness of her former promise, which the desire of exciting sympathy in those we esteem, and the melancholy pleasure which the heart finds in lingering among the scenes of former happiness, had induced her to give. She endeavoured to compose her spirits, which were agitated by the remembrance of past sufferings, and gave him a relation of the following circumstances.

CHAPTER VII

LOUISA, Baroness Malcolm, was the descendant of an ancient and honourable house in Switzerland. Her father, the Marquis de St. Claire, inherited all those brave qualities, and that stern virtue, which had so eminently distinguished his ancestors.* Early in life he lost a wife whom he tenderly loved, and he seemed to derive his sole consolation from the education of the dear children she had left behind. His son, whom he had brought up to the arms himself so honourably bore, fell before he reached his nineteenth year, in the service of his country; an elder daughter died in infancy; Louisa was his sole surviving child. His chateau was situated in one of those delightful vallies of the Swiss cantons, in which the beautiful and the sublime are so happily united; where the magnificent features of the scenery are contrasted, and their effect heightened by the blooming luxuriance of woods and pasturage, by the gentle winding of the stream, and the peaceful aspect of the cottage. The Marquis was now retired from the service, for grey age had overtaken him. His residence was the resort of foreigners of distinction, who, attracted by the united talents of the soldier and the philosopher, under his roof partook of the hospitality so characteristic of his country. Among the visitors of this description was the late Baron Malcolm, brother to the present Chief, who then travelled through Switzerland. The beauty of Louisa, embellished by the elegance of a mind highly cultivated, touched his heart, and he solicited her hand in marriage. The manly sense of the Baron, and the excellencies of his disposition, had not passed unobserved, or unapproved by the Marquis; while the graces of his person, and of his mind, had anticipated for him, in the heart of Louisa, a pre-eminence over every other suitor. The Marquis had but one objection to the marriage; this was likewise the objection of Louisa: neither the one nor the other could endure the idea of the distance which was to separate them. Louisa was to the Marquis the last prop of his declining years; the Marquis was to Louisa the father and the friend to whom her heart had hitherto been solely devoted, and from whom it could not now be torn but with an anguish equal to its attachment. This remained an insurmountable obstacle, till it was removed by the tenderness of the Baron, who entreated the Marquis to quit Switzerland, and reside with his daughter in Scotland. The attachment of the Marquis to his natal land, and the pride of hereditary dominion, was too powerful to suffer him to acquiesce in the proposal without much struggle of contending feelings. The desire of securing the happiness of his child, by a union with a character so excellent as the Baron's, and of seeing her settled before death should deprive her of the protection of a father, at length subdued every other consideration, and he resigned the hand of his daughter to the Baron Malcolm. The Marquis adjusted his affairs, and consigning his estates to the care of trusty agents, bade a last adieu to his beloved country; that country which, during sixty years, had been the principal scene of his happiness, and of his regrets. The course of years had not obliterated from his heart the early affections of his youth: he took a sad farewell of that grave which enclosed the reliques of his wife, from which it was not his least effort to depart, and whither he ordered that his remains should be conveyed. Louisa quitted Switzerland with a concern scarcely less acute than that of her father; the poignancy of which, however, was greatly softened by the tender assiduities of her Lord, whose affectionate attentions hourly heightened her esteem, and encreased* her love.

They arrived at Scotland without any accident, where the Baron welcomed Louisa as the mistress of his domains. The Marquis de St. Claire had apartments in the castle, where the evening of his days declined in peaceful happiness. Before his death, he had the pleasure of seeing his race renewed in the children of the Baroness, in a son who was called by the name of the Marquis, and in a daughter who now shared with her mother the sorrows of confinement. On the death of the Marquis it was necessary for the Baron to visit Switzerland, in order to take possession of his estates, and to adjust some affairs which a long absence had deranged. He attended the remains of the Marquis to their last abode. The Baroness, desirous of once more beholding her native country, and anxious to pay a last respect to the memory of her father, entrusted her children to the care of a faithful old servant, whom she had brought with her from the Vallois, and who had been the nurse of her early childhood, and accompanied the Baron to the continent. Having deposited the remains of the Marquis according to his wish in the tomb of his wife, and arranged their affairs, they returned to Scotland, where the first intelligence they received on their arrival at the castle, was of the death of their son, and of the old nurse his attendant. The servant had died soon after their departure; the child only a fortnight before their return. This disastrous event affected equally the Baron and his lady, who never ceased to condemn herself for having entrusted her son to the care of servants. Time, however subdued the poignancy of this affliction, but came fraught with another yet more acute; this was the death of the Baron, who, in the pride of youth, constituting the felicity of his family, and of his people, was killed by a fall from his horse, which he received in hunting. He left the Baroness and an only daughter to bewail with unceasing sorrow his loss.

The paternal estates devolved of course to his only brother, the present Baron, whose character formed a mournful and striking contrast to that of the deceased Lord. All his personal property, which was considerable, with the estates in Switzerland, he bequeathed to his beloved wife and daughter. The new Baron, immediately on the demise of his brother, took possession of the castle, but allowed the Baroness, with a part of her suit, to remain its inhabitant till the expiration of the year. The Baroness, absorbed in grief, still loved to recall, in the scene of her late felicity, the image of her Lord, and to linger in his former haunts. This motive, together with the necessity of preparation for a journey to Switzerland, induced her to accept the offer of the Baron.

The memory of his brother had quickly faded from the mind of Malcolm, whose attention appeared to be wholly occupied by schemes of avarice and ambition. His arrogance, and boundless love of power, embroiled him with the neighbouring Chiefs, and engaged him in continual hostility. He seldom visited the

Baroness; when he did, his manner was cold, and even haughty. The Baroness, shocked to receive such treatment from the brother of her deceased Lord, and reduced to feel herself an unwelcome guest in that castle which she had been accustomed to consider as her own, determined to set off for the continent immediately, and seek, in the solitudes of her native mountains, an asylum from the frown of insulting power. The contrast of character between the brothers drew many a sigh of bitter recollection from her heart, and added weight to the sorrows which already oppressed it. She gave orders, therefore, to her domestics, to prepare for immediate departure; but was soon after told that the Baron had forbade them to obey the command. Astonished at this circumstance, she had not time to demand an explanation, ere a message from Malcolm required a few moments private conversation. The messenger was followed almost instantly by the Baron, who entered the apartment with hurried steps, his countenance overspread with the dark purposes of his soul. 'I come, Madam,' said he, in a voice stern and determined, 'to inform you, that you quit not this castle. The estates which you call yours, are mine; and think not that I shall neglect to prosecute my claim. The frequent and ill-timed generosities of my brother, have diminished the value of the lands which are mine by inheritance; and I have therefore an indispensable right to repay myself from those estates which he acquired with you. In point of justice, he possessed not the right of devising these estates, and I shall not suffer myself to be deceived by the evasions of the law; resign, therefore, the will, which remains only a record of unjust wishes, and ineffectual claims. When the receipts from your estates have satisfied my demands, they shall again be yours. The apartments you now inhabit shall remain your own; but beyond the wall of this castle you shall not pass; for I will not, by suffering your departure, afford you an opportunity of contesting those rights which I can enforce without opposition.'

Overcome with astonishment and dread, the Baroness was for some time deprived of all power of reply. At length, roused by the spirit of indignation, 'I am too well informed, my Lord,' said she, 'of my just claims to the lands in question; and know also too well the value of that integrity which is now no more, to credit your bold assertions; they serve only to unveil to me the darkness of a character, cruel and rapacious; whose boundless avarice, trampling on the barriers of justice and humanity, seizes on the right of the defenceless widow, and on the portion of the unresisting orphan. This, my Lord, you are permitted to do; they have no means of resistance; but think not to impose on me by a sophistical assertion of right, or to gloss the villainy of your conduct with the colours of justice; the artifice is beneath the desperate force of your character, and is not sufficiently specious to deceive the discernment of virtue. From being your prisoner I have no means of escaping; but never, my Lord, will I resign into your hands that will which is the efficient* bond of my rights, and the last sad record of the affection of my departed Lord.' Grief closed her lips. The Baron denouncing vengeance on her resistance, his features inflamed with rage, quitted the apartment. The Baroness was left to lament, with deepening anguish, the stroke which had deprived her of a beloved husband; and reflection gave her the wretchedness of her situation in yet more lively colours. She was now a stranger in a foreign land, deprived by him, of whom she had a right to demand protection, of all her possessions; a prisoner in his castle, without one friend to vindicate her cause, and far remote from any means of appeal to the laws of the country. She wept over the youthful Laura, and while she pressed her with mournful fondness to her bosom, she was confirmed in her resolution never to relinquish that will, by which alone the rights of her injured child could ever be ascertained.

The Baron, bold in iniquity, obtained, by forged powers, the revenues of the foreign estates; and by this means, effectually kept the Baroness in his power, and deprived her of her last resource. Secure in the possession of the estates, and of the Baroness, he no longer regarded the will as an object of importance; and as she did not attempt any means of escape, or the recovery of her rights, he suffered her to remain undisturbed, and in quiet possession of the will.

The Baroness now passed her days in unvaried sorrow, except in those intervals when she forced her mind from its melancholy subject, and devoted herself to the education of her daughter. The artless efforts of Laura, to assuage the sorrows of her mother, only fixed them in her heart in deeper impression, since they gave to her mind, in stronger tints, the cruelty and oppression to which her tender years were condemned. The progress which she made in music and drawing, and in the lighter subjects of literature, while it pleased the Baroness, who was her sole instructress, brought with it the bitter apprehension, that these accomplishments would probably be buried in the obscurity of a prison; still, however, they were not useless, since they served at present to cheat affliction of many a weary moment, and would in future delude the melancholy hours of solitude. Laura was particularly fond of the lute, which she touched with exquisite sensibility, and whose tender notes were so sweetly in unison with the chords of sorrow, and with those plaintive tones with which she loved to accompany it. While she sung, the Baroness would sit absorbed in recollection, the tears fast falling from her eyes, and she might be said to taste in those moments the luxury of woe.

Malcolm, stung with a sense of guilt, avoided the presence of his injured captive, and sought an asylum from conscience in the busy scenes of war.

Eighteen years had now elapsed since the death of the Baron, and the confinement of Louisa. Time had blunted the point of affliction, though it still retained its venom; but she seldom dared to hope for that which for eighteen years had been withheld. She derived her only consolation from the improvement and the tender sympathy of her daughter, who endeavoured, by every soothing attention, to alleviate the sorrows of her parent.

It was at this period that the Baroness communicated to the Earl the story of her calamities

The Earl listened with deep attention to the recital. His soul burned with indignation against the Baron, while his heart gave to the sufferings of the fair mourners all that sympathy could ask. Yet he was relieved from a very painful sensation, when he learned that the beauty of Laura had not influenced the conduct of the Baron. Her oppressed situation struck upon his heart the finest touch of pity; and the passion which her beauty and her simplicity had inspired, was strengthened and meliorated by her misfortunes. The fate of his father, and the idea of his own injuries, rushed upon his mind; and, combining with the sufferings of the victims now before him, roused in his soul a storm of indignation, little inferior to that he had suffered in his first interview with the Baron. Every consideration sunk before the impulse of a just revenge; his mind, occupied with the hateful image of the murderer was hardened against danger, and in the first energies of his resentment he would have rushed to the apartment of Malcolm, and striking the sword of justice in his heart, have delivered the earth from a monster, and have resigned himself the willing sacrifice of the action. 'Shall the monster live?' cried he, rising from his seat. His step was hurried, and his countenance was stamped with a stern virtue. The Baroness was alarmed, and following him to the door of her apartment, which he had half opened, conjured him to pause for a moment on the dangers that surrounded him. The voice of reason, in the accents of the Baroness, interrupted the hurried tumult of his soul; the illusions of passion disappeared; he recollected that he was ignorant of the apartment of the Baron, and that he had no weapon to assist his purpose; and he found himself as a traveller on enchanted ground, when the wand of the magician suddenly dissolves the airy scene, and leaves him environed with the horrors of solitude and of darkness.

The Earl returned to his seat hopeless and dejected, and lost to every thing but to the bitterness of disappointment. He forgot where he was, and the lateness of the hour, till reminded by the Baroness of the dangers of a longer stay, when he mournfully bade her good night; and advancing to Laura with timid respect, pressed her hand tenderly to his lips, and retired to his prison.

CHAPTER VIII

HE had now opened the partition, and was entering the room, when by the faint gleam which the fire threw across the apartment, he perceived indistinctly the figure of a man, and in the same instant heard the sound of approaching armour. Surprize and horror thrilled through every nerve; he remained fixed to the spot, and for some moments hesitated whether to retire. A fearful silence ensued; the person whom he thought he had seen, disappeared in the darkness of the room; the noise of armour was heard no more; and he began to think that the figure he had seen, and the sound he had heard were the phantoms of a sick imagination, which the agitation of his spirits, the solemnity of the hour, and the wide desolation of the place, had conjured up. The low sounds of an unknown voice now started upon his ear; it seemed to be almost close beside him; he sprung onward, and his hand grasped the steely coldness of armour, while the arm it enclosed struggled to get free. 'Speak! what wretch art thou?' cried Osbert, when a sudden blaze of light from the fire discovered to him a soldier of the Baron. His agitation for some time prevented his observing that there was more of alarm than of design expressed in the countenance of the man; but the apprehension of the Earl was quickly lost in astonishment, when he beheld the guard at his feet. It was Edmund who had entered the prison under pretence of carrying fuel to the fire, but secretly for the purpose of conferring with Osbert. When the Earl understood he came from Alleyn, his bosom glowed with gratitude towards that generous youth, whose steady and active zeal had never relaxed since the hour in which he first engaged in his cause. The transport of his heart may be easily imagined, when he learned the schemes that were planning for his deliverance. The circumstance which had nearly defeated the warm hopes of his friends, was by him disregarded, since the knowledge of the secret door opened to him, with the assistance of a guide through the intricacies of the castle, a certain means of escape. Edmund was well acquainted with all these. The Earl told him of the discovery of the false pannel; bade him return to Alleyn with the joyful intelligence, and on his next night of watch prepare to aid him in escape. Edmund knew well the apartments which Osbert described, and the great staircase which led into a part of the castle that had long been totally forsaken, and from whence it was easy to pass unobserved into the vaults which communicated with the subterraneous passages in the rock.

Alleyn heard the report of James with a warm and generous joy, which impelled him to hasten immediately to the castle of Athlin, and dispel the sorrows that inhabited there; but the consideration that his sudden absence from the camp might create suspicion, and invite discovery, checked the impulse; and he yielded with reluctance to the necessity which condemned the Countess and Mary to the horrors of a lengthened suspense.

The Countess, meanwhile, whose designs, strengthened by the steady determination of Mary, were unshaken by the message of the Earl, which she considered as only the effect of a momentary impulse, watched the gradual departure of those days which led to that which enveloped the fate of her children, with agony and fainting hope. She received no news from the camp; no words of comfort from Alleyn; and she saw the confidence which had nourished her existence slowly sinking in despair. Mary sought to administer that comfort to the afflictions of her mother, which her own equally demanded; she strove, by the fortitude with which she endeavoured to resign herself, to soften the asperity of the sufferings which threatened the Countess, and she contemplated the approaching storm with the determined coolness of a mind aspiring to virtue as the chief good. But she sedulously sought to exclude Alleyn from her mind; his disinterested and noble conduct excited emotions dangerous to her fortitude, and which rendered yet more poignant the tortures of the approaching sacrifice.

Anxious to inform the Baroness of his approaching deliverance, to assure her of his best services, to bid adieu to Laura, and to seize the last opportunity he might ever possess of disclosing to her his admiration and his love, the Earl revisited the apartments of the Baroness. She felt a lively pleasure on the prospect of his escape; and Laura, in the joy which animated her on hearing this intelligence, forgot the sorrows of her own situation; forgot that of which her heart soon reminded her—that Osbert was leaving the place of her confinement, and that she should probably see him no more. This thought cast a sudden shade over her features, and from the enlivening expression of joy, they resumed their wonted melancholy. Osbert marked the momentary change, and his heart spoke to him the occasion. 'My cup of joy is dashed with bitterness,' said he, 'for amid the happiness of approaching deliverance, I quit not my prison without some pangs of keen regret;—pangs which it were probably useless to make known, yet which my feeling will not suffer me at this moment to conceal. Within these walls, from whence I fly with eagerness, I leave a heart fraught with the most tender passion;—a heart which, while it beats with life, must ever unite the image of Laura with the fondness of love. Could I hope that she were not insensible to my attachment I should depart in peace, and would defy the obstacles which bid me despair. Were I even certain that she would repel my love with cold indifference, I would yet, if she accept my services, effect her rescue, or give my life the forfeiture.' Laura was silent; she wished to speak her gratitude, yet feared to tell her love; but the soft timidity of her eye, and the tender glow of her cheek, revealed the secret that trembled on her lips. The Baroness observed her confusion, and thanking the Earl for the noble service he offered, declined accepting it. She besought him to involve no further the peace of his family and of himself, by attempting an enterprize so crowded with dangers, and which might probably cost him his life. The arguments of the Baroness fell forceless when opposed to the feelings of the Earl; so warmly he urged his suit, and dwelt so forcibly on his approaching departure, that the Baroness ceased to oppose, and the silence of Laura yielded acquiescence. After a tender farewell, with many earnest wishes for his safety, the Earl quitted the apartment elated with hope. But the Baron had been informed of his projected escape, and had studied the means of counteracting it. The centinel had communicated his discovery to some of his comrades, who, without virtue or courage sufficient to quit the service of the Baron, were desirous of obtaining his favour and failed not to seize on an opportunity so flattering as the present, to accomplish their purpose they communicated to their Chief the intelligence they had received.

Malcolm, careful to conceal his knowledge of the scheme, from a design to entrap those of the clan who were to meet the Earl, had suffered Edmund to return to his station at the prison, where he had placed the informers as secret guards, and had taken such other precautions as were necessary to intercept their flight, should they elude the vigilance of the soldiers, and likewise to secure those of his people who should be drawn toward the castle in expectation of their Chief. Having done this, he prided himself in security, and in the certainty of exulting over his enemies, thus entangled in their own stratagem.

After many weary moments of impatience to Alleyn, and of expectation to the Earl, the night at length arrived on which hung the event of all their hopes. It was agreed that Alleyn, with a chosen few, should await the arrival of the Earl in the cavern where terminated the subterraneous avenue. Alleyn parted from James with extreme agitation, and returned to his tent to compose his mind.

It was now the dead of night; profound sleep reigned through the castle of Dunbayne, when Edmund gently unbolted the prison door, and hailed the Earl. He sprung forward, and instantly unclosed the pannel, which they fastened after them to prevent discovery, and passing with fearful steps the cold and silent apartments, descended the great stair-case into the hall, whose wide and dark desolation was rendered visible only by the dim light of the taper which Edmund carried in his hand, and whose vaulted ceiling re-echoed their steps. After various windings they descended into the vaults; in passing their dreary length they often paused in fearful silence, listening to the hollow blasts which burst suddenly through the passages, and which seemed to bear in the sound the footsteps of pursuit. At length they reached the extremity of the vaults, where Edmund searched for a trap-door which lay almost concealed in the dirt and darkness; after some time they found, and with difficulty raised it, for it was long since it had been opened; and it was besides heavy with iron work. They entered, and letting the door fall after them, descended a narrow flight of steps which conducted them to a winding passage closed by a door that opened into the main avenue whence Alleyn had before made his escape. Having gained this, they stepped on with confidence, for they were now not far from the cavern where Alleyn and his companions were awaiting their arrival. The heart of Alleyn now swelled with joy, for he perceived a gleam of distant light break upon the walls of the avenue, and at the same time thought he heard the faint sound of approaching footsteps. Impatient to throw himself at the feet of the Earl, he entered the avenue. The light grew stronger upon the walls; but a point of rock, whose projection caused a winding in the passage, concealed from his view the persons his eyes so eagerly sought. The sound of steps was now fast approaching, and Alleyn gaining the rock, suddenly turned upon three soldiers of the Baron. They instantly seized him their prisoner. Astonishment for a while overcame every other sensation; but as they led him along, the horrid reverse of the moment struck upon his heart with all its consequences, and he had no doubt that the Earl had been seized and carried back to his prison. As he marched along, absorbed in this reflection, a light appeared at some distance, from a door that opened upon the avenue, and discovered the figures of two men, who on perceiving the party, they retreated with precipitation, and closed the door after them. Alleyn knew the Earl in the person of one of them. Two of the soldiers quitting Alleyn, pursued the fugitives, and quickly disappeared through a door. Alleyn finding himself alone with the guard, seized the moment of opportunity, and made a desperate effort to regain his sword. He succeeded; and in the suddenness of the attack, obtained also the weapon of his adversary, who, unarmed, fell at his feet, and called for mercy. Alleyn gave him his life. The soldier, grateful for the gift, and fearful of the Baron's vengeance, desired to fly with him, and enlist in his service. They quitted the subterraneous way together. On entering the cavern, Alleyn found it vacated by his friends, who on hearing the clash of armour, and the loud and menacing voices of the soldiers, understood his fate, and apprehensive of numbers, had fled to avoid a similar disaster. Alleyn returned to his tent, shocked with disappointment, and lost in despair. Every effort which he had made for the deliverance of the Earl, had proved unsuccessful; and this scheme, on which was suspended his last hope, had been defeated at the very moment when he exulted in its completion. He threw himself on the ground, and lost in bitter thought, observed not the curtain of his tent undraw, till recalled by a sudden noise, he looked up, and beheld the Earl. Terror fixed him to the spot, and for a moment he involuntarily acknowledged the traditionary visions of his nation.* The well-known voice of Osbert, however, awakened him to truth, and the ardor with which he embraced his knees, immediately convinced him that he clasped reality.

The soldiers, in the eagerness of pursuit, had mistaken the door by which Osbert had retired, and had entered one below it, which, after engaging them in a fruitless search through various intricate passages, had conducted them to a remote part of the castle, from whence, after much perplexity and loss of time, they were at length extricated. The Earl, who had retreated on sight of the soldiers, had fled in the mean time to regain the trap-door; but the united strength of himself and of Edmund was in vain exerted to open it. Compelled to encounter the approaching evil, the Earl took the sword of his companion, resolving to meet the approach of his adversaries, and to effect his deliverance, or yield his life and his misfortunes to the attempt. With this design he advanced deliberately along the passage, and arriving at the door, stopped to discover the motions of his pursuers: all was profoundly silent. After remaining some time in this situation, he opened the door, and examining the avenue with a firm yet anxious eye as far as the light of his taper threw its beams, discovered no human being. He proceeded with cautious firmness towards the cavern, every instant expecting the soldiers to start suddenly upon him from some dark recess.—With astonishment he reached the cave without interruption; and unable to account for his unexpected deliverance, hastened with Edmund to join his faithful people.

The soldiers who watched the prison, being ignorant of any other way by which the Earl could escape, than the door which they guarded, had suffered Edmund to enter the apartment without fear. It was some time before they discovered their error; surprized at the length of his stay, they opened the door of the prison, which to their utter astonishment, they found empty. The grates were examined; they remained as usual; every corner was explored; but the false pannel remained unknown; and having finished their examination without discovering any visible means by which the Earl had quitted the prison, they were seized with terror, concluding it to be the work of a super-natural power, and immediately alarmed the castle. The Baron, roused by the tumult, was informed of the fact, and dubious of the integrity of his guards, ascended to the apartment; which having himself examined without discovering any means of escape, he no longer hesitated to pronounce the centinels access-ary to the Earl's enlargement. The unfeigned terror which they exhibited was mistaken for artifice, and their supposed treachery was admitted and punished in the same moment. They were thrown into the dungeon of the castle. Soldiers were immedi-ately dispatched in pursuit; but the time which had elapsed ere the guards had entered the prison, had given the Earl an oppor-tunity of escape. When the certainty of this was communicated to the Baron, every passion whose single force is misery, united in his breast to torture him; and his brain, exasperated almost to madness, gave him only direful images of revenge.

The Baroness and Laura, awakened by the tumult, had been filled with apprehension for the Earl, till they were informed of the cause of the general confusion; and hope and dubious* joy were ere long confirmed into certainty, for they were told of the fruitless search of the pursuers.

It was now the last day of the term in which the Countess had stipulated to return her answer; she had yet heard nothing from Alleyn; for Alleyn had been busied in schemes, of the event of which he could send no account, for their success had been yet undetermined. Every hope of the Earl's deliverance was now expired, and in the anguish of her heart, the Countess prepared to give that answer which would send the devoted Mary to the arms of the murderer. Mary, who assumed a fortitude not her own, strove to abate the rigor of her mother's sufferings, but vainly strove; they were of a nature which defied consolation.

She wrote the fatal agreement, but delayed till the last moment delivering it into the hands of the messenger. It was necessary, however, that the Baron should receive it on the following morn, lest the impatience of revenge should urge him to seize on the life of the Earl as the forfeiture of delay. She sent, therefore, for the messenger, who was a veteran of the clan, and with extreme agitation delivered to him her answer; grief interrupted her voice; she was unable to speak to him; and he was awaiting her orders, when the door of the apartment was thrown open, and the Earl, followed by Alleyn, threw himself at her feet. A faint scream was uttered by the Countess, and she sunk in her chair. Mary, not daring to trust herself with the delightful vision, endeavoured to restrain the tide of joy, which hurried to her heart, and threatened to overwhelm her.

The castle of Athlin resounded with tumultuous joy on this happy event; the courts were filled with those of the clan who had been disabled from attending the field, and whom the report of the Earl's return, which had circulated with astonishing rapidity, had brought thither. The hall re-echoed with voices; and the people could hardly be restrained from rushing into the presence of their Chief, to congratulate him on his escape.

When the first transports of the meeting were subsided, the Earl presented Alleyn to his family as his friend and deliverer; whose steady attachment he could never forget, and whose zealous services he could never repay. The cheek of Mary glowed with pleasure and gratitude at this tribute to the worth of Alleyn; and the smiling approbation of her eyes rewarded him for his noble deeds. The Countess received him as the deliverer of both her children, and related to Osbert the adventure in the wood. The Earl embraced Alleyn, who received the united acknowledgments of the family, with unaffected modesty. Osbert hesitated not to pronounce the Baron the author of the plot; his heart swelled to avenge the repeated injuries of his family, and he secretly resolved to challenge the enemy to single combat.* To renew the siege he considered as a vain project; and this challenge, though a very inadequate mode of revenge, was the only honourable one that remained for him. He forbore to mention his design to the Countess, well knowing that her tenderness would oppose the measure, and throw difficulties in his way, which would embarrass, without preventing his purpose. He mentioned the misfortunes of the Baroness, and the loveliness of her daughter, and excited the esteem and the commiseration of his hearers.

The clamours of the people to behold their Lord, now arose to the apartment of the Countess, and he descended into the hall, accompanied by Alleyn, to gratify their zeal. An universal shout of joy resounded through the walls on his appearance. A noble pleasure glowed on the countenance of the Earl at sight of his faithful people; and in the delight of that moment his heart bore testimony to the superior advantages of an equitable government. The Earl, impatient to testify his gratitude, introduced Alleyn to the clan, as his friend and deliverer, and immediately presented his father with a lot of land, where he might end his days in peace and plenty. Old Alleyn thanked the Earl for his offered kindness, but declined accepting it; alledging, that he was attached to his old cottage, and that he had already sufficient for the comforts of his age.

On the following morning, a messenger was privately dispatched to the Baron, with the challenge of the Earl. The challenge was couched in terms of haughty indignation, and expressed, that nothing but the failure of all other means could have urged him to the condescension of meeting the assassin of his father, on terms of equal combat.

Happiness was once more restored to Athlin. The Countess, in the unexpected preservation of her children, seemed to be alive only to joy. The Earl was now for a time secure in the bosom of his family, and, though his impatience to avenge the injuries of those most dear to him, and to snatch from the hand of oppression the fair sufferers at Dunbayne, would not allow him to be tranquil, yet he assumed a gaiety unknown to his heart, and the days were spent in festivals and joy.

CHAPTER IX

IT was at this period, that, one stormy evening, the Countess was sitting with her family in a room, the windows of which looked upon the sea.* The winds burst in sudden squalls over the deep, and dashed the foaming waves against the rocks with inconceivable fury. The spray, notwithstanding the high situation of the castle, flew up with violence against the windows. The Earl went out upon the terrace beneath to contemplate the storm. The moon shone faintly by intervals, through broken clouds upon the waters, illumining the white foam which burst around, and enlightening the scene sufficiently to render it visible. The surges broke on the distant shores in deep resounding murmurs, and the solemn pauses between the stormy gusts filled the mind with enthusiastic awe.* As the Earl stood wrapt in the sublimity of the scene, the moon, suddenly emerging from a heavy cloud, shewed him at some distance a vessel driven by the fury of the blast towards the coast. He presently heard the signals of distress; and soon after shrieks of terror, and a confused uproar of voices were borne on the wind. He hastened from the terrace to order his people to go out with boats to the assistance of the crew, for he doubted not that the vessel was wrecked; but the sea ran so high as to make the adventure impracticable. The sound of voices ceased, and he concluded that the wretched mariners were lost, when the screams of distress again struck his ear, and again were lost in the tumult of the storm; in a moment after, the vessel struck upon the rock beneath the castle; an universal shriek ensued. The Earl, with his people, hastened to the assistance of the crew; the fury of the gust was now abated, and the Earl, jumping into a boat with Alleyn and some others, rowed to the ship, where they rescued a part of the drowning people. They were conducted to the castle, and every comfort was liberally administered to them. Among those, whom the Earl had received into his boat, was a stranger, whose dignified aspect and manners bespoke him to be of rank; he had several people belonging to him, but they were foreigners, and ignorant of the language of the country. He thanked his deliverer with a noble frankness, that charmed him. In the hall they were met by the Countess and her daughter, who received the stranger with the warm welcome, which compassion for his situation had inspired. He was conducted to the supper room, where the magnificence of the board exhibited only the usual hospitality of his host. The stranger spoke English fluently, and displayed in his conversation a manly and vigorous mind, acquainted with the sciences, and with life; and the cast of his observations seemed to characterize the benevolence of his heart. The Earl was so much pleased with his guest, that he pressed him to remain at his castle till another vessel could be procured; his guest equally pleased with the Earl, and a stranger to the country, accepted the invitation.

New distress now broke upon the peace of Athlin; several days had expired, and the messenger, who had been sent to Malcolm, did not appear. It was almost evident, that the Baron, disappointed and enraged at the escape of his prisoner, and eager for a sacrifice, had seized this man as the subject of a paltry revenge. The Earl, however, resolved to wait a few days, and watch the event.

The struggles of latent tenderness and assumed indifference, banished tranquillity from the bosom of Mary, and pierced it with many sorrows. The friendship and honours bestowed by the Earl on Alleyn, who now resided solely at the castle, touched her heart with a sweet pride; but alas! these distinctions served only to confirm her admiration of that worth, which had already attached her affections, and afforded him opportunities of exhibiting, in brighter colours, the various excellencies of a heart noble and expansive, and of a mind, whose native elegance meliorated and adorned the bold vigour of its flights. The langour of melancholy, notwithstanding the efforts of Mary, would at intervals steal from beneath the disguise of chearfulness, and diffuse over her beautiful features an expression extremely interesting. The stranger was not insensible to its charms, and it served to heighten the admiration, with which he had first beheld her, into something more tender and more powerful. The modest dignity, with which she delivered her sentiments, which breathed the purest delicacy and benevolence, touched his heart, and he felt an interest concerning her, which he had never before experienced.

Alleyn, whose heart amid the anxieties and tumults of the past scenes, had still sighed to the image of Mary;—that image, which fancy had pictured in all the charms of the original, and whose glowing tints were yet softened and rendered more interesting by the shade of melancholy with which absence and a hopeless passion had surrounded them, found, amid the leisure of peace, and the frequent opportunities which were afforded him of beholding the object of his attachment, his sighs redouble, and the glooms of sorrow thicken. In the presence of Mary, a soft sadness clouded his brow; he endeavoured to assume a cheerfulness foreign to his heart; but endeavoured in vain. Mary perceived the change in his manners; and the observation did not contribute to enliven her own. The Earl, too, observed that Alleyn had lost much of his wonted spirits, and bantered him on the change, but thought not of his sister.

Alleyn wished to quit a place so destructive to his peace as the castle of Athlin; he formed repeated resolutions of withdrawing himself from those walls, which held him in a sort of fascination, and rendered ineffectual every half-formed wish, and every weak endeavour. When he could no longer behold Mary, he would frequently retire to the terrace, which was overlooked by the windows of her apartment, and spend half the night in traversing, with silent, mournful steps, that spot, which afforded him the melancholy pleasure of being near the object of his love.

Matilda wished to question Alleyn concerning some circumstances of the late events, and for this purpose ordered him one day to attend her in her closet. As he passed the outer apartment of the Countess, he perceived something lying near the door, through which she had before gone, and, examining it, discovered a bracelet, to which was attached a miniature of Mary. His heart beat quick at the sight; the temptation was too powerful to be resisted; he concealed it in his bosom, and passed on. On quitting the closet, he sought, with breathless impatience, a spot, where he might contemplate at leisure that precious portrait, which chance had so kindly thrown in his way. He drew it trembling from his bosom, and beheld again that countenance, whose sweet expression had touched his heart with all the delightful agonies of love. As he pressed it with impassioned tenderness to his lips, the tear of rapture trembled in his eye, and the romantic ardour of the moment was scarcely heightened by the actual presence of the beloved object, whose light step now stole upon his ear, and half turning he beheld not the picture, but the reality!—Surprized!—confused!—The picture fell from his hand. Mary, who had accidentally strolled to that spot, on observing the agitation of Alleyn, was retiring, when he, in whose heart had been awakened every tender sensation, losing in the temptation of the moment the fear of disdain, and forgetting the resolution which he had formed of eternal silence, threw himself at her feet, and pressed her hand to his trembling lips. His tongue would have told her that he loved, but his emotion, and the repulsive look of Mary, prevented him. She instantly disengaged herself with an air of offended dignity, and casting on him a look of mingled anger and concern, withdrew in silence. Alleyn remained fixed to the spot; his eyes pursuing her retiring steps, insensible to every feeling but those of love and despair. So absorbed was he in the transition of the moment, that he almost doubted whether a visionary illusion had not crossed his sight to blast his only remaining comfort—the consciousness of deserving, and of possessing the esteem of her he loved. He left the place with anguish in his heart, and, in the perturbation of his mind, forgot the picture.

Mary had observed her mother's bracelet fall from his hand, and was no longer in perplexity concerning her miniature; but in the confusion which his behaviour occasioned her, she forgot to demand it of him. The Countess had missed it almost immediately after his departure from the closet, and had caused a search to be made, which proving fruitless, her suspicions wavered upon him. The Earl, who soon after passed the spot whence Alleyn had just departed, found the miniature. It was not long ere Alleyn recollected the treasure he had dropped, and returned in search of it. Instead of the picture, he found the Earl: a conscious blush crossed his cheek; the confusion of his countenance informed Osbert of a part of the truth; who, anxious to know by what means he had obtained it, presented him the picture, and demanded if he knew it. The soul of Alleyn knew not to dissemble; he acknowledged that he had found, and concealed it; prompted by that passion, the confession of which, no other circumstance than the present could have wrung from his heart. The Earl listened to him with a mixture of concern and pity; but hereditary pride chilled the warm feelings of friendship and of gratitude, and extinguished the faint spark of hope which the discovery had kindled in the bosom of Alleyn. 'Fear not, my Lord,' said he, 'the degradation of your house from one who would sacrifice his life in its defence; never more shall the passion which glows in my heart escape from my lips. I will retire from the spot where I have buried my tranquillity.' 'No,' replied the Earl, 'you shall remain here; I can confide in your honour. O! that the only reward which is adequate to your worth and to your services, it should be impossible for me to bestow.' His voice faultered, and he turned away to conceal his emotion, with a suffering little inferior to that of Alleyn.

The discovery which Mary had made, did not contribute to restore peace to her mind. Every circumstance conspired to assure her of that ardent passion which filled the bosom of him whom all her endeavours could not teach her to forget; and this conviction served only to heighten her malady, and consequently her wretchedness.

The interest which the stranger discovered, and the attention he paid to Mary, had not passed unobserved by Alleyn. Love pointed to him the passion which was rising in his heart, and whispered that the vows of his rival would be propitious. The words of Osbert confirmed him in the torturing apprehension; for though his humble birth had never suffered him to hope, yet he thought he discovered in the speech of the Earl, something more than mere hereditary pride.

The stranger had contemplated the lovely form of Mary with increasing admiration, since the first hour he beheld her; this admiration was now confirmed into love;—and he resolved to acquaint the Earl with his birth, and with his passion. For this purpose, he one morning drew him aside to the terrace of the castle, where they could converse without interruption; and pointing to the ocean, over which he had so lately been borne, thanked the Earl, who had thus softened the horrors of shipwreck, and the desolation of a foreign land, by the kindness of his hospitality. He informed him that he was a native of Switzerland, where he possessed confiderable estates, from which he bore the title of Count de Santmorin; that enquiry of much moment to his interests had brought him to Scotland, to a neighbouring port of which he was bound, when the disaster from which he had been so happily rescued, arrested the progress of his designs. He then related to the Earl, that his voyage was undertaken upon a report of the death of some relations, at whose demise considerable estates in Switzerland became his inheritance. That the income of these estates had been hitherto received upon the authority of powers, which, if the report was true, were become invalid.

The Earl listened to this narrative in silent astonishment, and enquired, with much emotion, the name of the Count's relations. 'The Baroness Malcolm,' returned he. The Earl clasped his hands in extasy. The Count, surprized at his agitation, began to fear that the Earl was disagreeably interested in the welfare of his adversaries, and regretted that he had disclosed the affair, till he observed the pleasure which was diffused through his features. Osbert explained the cause of his emotion, by relating his knowledge of the Baroness; in the progress of whose story, the character of Malcolm was sufficiently elucidated. He told the cause of his hatred towards the Baron, and the history of his imprisonment; and also confided to his honour the secret of his challenge.

The indignation of the Count was strongly excited; he was, however, prevailed on by Osbert to forego any immediate effort of revenge, awaiting for awhile the movements of Malcolm.

The Count was so absorbed in wonder and in new sensations, that he had almost forgot the chief object of the interview. Recollecting himself, he discovered his passion, and requested permission of the Earl to throw himself at the feet of Mary. The Earl listened to the declaration with a mixture of pleasure and concern; the remembrance of Alleyn saddened his mind; but the wish of an equal connection, made him welcome the offers of the Count, whose alliance, he told him, would do honour to the first nobility of his nation. If he found the sentiments of his sister in sympathy with his own on this point, he would welcome him to his family with the affection of a brother; but he wished to discover the situation of her heart, ere his noble friend disclosed to her his prepossession.

The Earl on his return to the castle enquired for Mary, whom he found in the apartment of her mother. He opened to them the history of the Count; his relationship with the Baroness Malcolm, with the object of his expedition, and closed the narrative with discovering the attachment of his friend to Mary, and his offers of alliance with his family. Mary grew pale at this declaration; there was a pang in her heart which would not suffer her to speak; she threw her eyes on the ground, and burst into tears. The Earl took her hand tenderly in his; 'My beloved sister,' said he, 'knows me too well to doubt my affection, or to suppose I can wish to influence her upon a subject so material to her future happiness; and where her heart ought to be the principal directress. Do me the justice to believe, that I make known to you the offers of the Count as a friend, not as a director. He is a man, who from the short period of our acquaintance, I have judged to be deserving of particular esteem. His mind appears to be noble; his heart expansive; his rank is equal with your own; and he loves you with an attachment warm and sincere. But with all these advantages, I would not have my sister give herself to the man who does not meet an interest in her heart to plead his cause.'

The gentle soul of Mary swelled with gratitude towards her brother; she would have thanked him for the tenderness of these sentiments, but a variety of emotions were struggling at her heart, and suppressed her utterance; tears and a smile, softly clouded with sorrow, were all she could give him in reply. He could not but perceive that some secret cause of grief preyed upon her mind, and he solicited to know, and to remove it. 'My dear brother will believe the gratitude which his kindness—.' She would have finished the sentence, but the words died away upon her lips, and she threw herself on the bosom of her mother, endeavouring to conceal her distress, and wept in silence. The

Countess too well understood the grief of her daughter; she had witnessed the secret struggles of her heart, which all her endeavours were not able to overcome, and which rendered the offers of the Count disgusting, and dreadful to her imagination. Matilda knew how to feel for her sufferings; but the affection of the mother extended her views beyond the present temporary evil, to the future welfare of her child; and in the long perspective of succeeding years, she beheld her united to the Count, whose character diffused happiness, and the mild dignity of virtue to all around him: she received the thanks of Mary for her gentle guidance to the good she possessed; the artless looks of the little ones around her, smiled their thanks; and the luxury of that scene recalled the memory of times for ever passed, and mingled with the tear of rapture the sigh of fond regret. The surest method of erasing that impression which threatened serious evil to the peace of her child if suffered to continue, and to secure her permanent felicity, was to unite her to the Count; whose amiable disposition would soon win her affections, and obliterate from her heart every improper remembrance of Alleyn. She determined, therefore, to employ argument and gentle persuasion, to guide her to her purpose. She knew the mind of Mary to be delicate and candid; easy of conviction, and firm to pursue what her judgment approved; and she did not despair of succeeding.

The Earl still pressed to know the cause of that emotion which afflicted her. 'I am unworthy of your solicitude,' said Mary, 'I cannot teach my heart to submit.' 'To submit!—Can you suppose your friends can wish your heart to submit on a point so material to its happiness, to aught that is repugnant to its feelings? If the offers of the Count are displeasing to you, tell me so; and I will return him his answer. Believe that my first wish is to see you happy.' 'Generous Osbert! How can I repay the goodness of such a brother! I would accept in gratitude the hand of the Count, did not my feelings assure me I should be miserable. I admire his character, and esteem his goodness; but alas!—why should I conceal it from you?—My heart is another's—is another's, whose noble deeds have won its involuntary regards; and who is yet unconscious of my distinction, one who shall for ever remain in ignorance of it.' The idea of Alleyn flashed into the mind of the Earl, and he no longer doubted to whom her heart was engaged. 'My own sentiments,' said he, 'sufficiently inform me of the object of your admiration. You do well to remember the dignity of your sex and of your rank; though I must lament with you, that worth like Alleyn's is not impowered by fortune to take its standard with nobility.' At Alleyn's name, the blushes of Mary confirmed Osbert in his discovery. 'My child,' said the Countess, 'will not resign her tranquillity to a vain and ignoble attachment. She may esteem merit wherever it is found, but she will remember the duty which she owes to her family and to herself, in contracting an alliance which is to support or diminish the ancient consequence of her house. The offers of a man endowed with so much apparent excellence as the Count, and whose birth is equal to your own, affords a prospect too promising of felicity, to be hastily rejected. We will hereafter converse more largely on this subject.' 'Never shall you have reason to blush for your daughter,' said Mary, with a modest pride; 'but pardon me, Madam, if I entreat that we no more renew a subject so painful to my feelings, and which cannot be productive of good;—for never will I give my hand where my heart does not accompany it.' This was not a time to press the topic; the Countess for the present desisted, and the Earl left the apartment with a heart divided between pity and disappointment. Hope, however, whispered to his wishes, that Mary might in time be induced to admit the addresses of the Count, and he determined not wholly to destroy his hopes.

CHAPTER X

THE Count was walking on the ramparts of the castle, involved in thought, when Osbert approached; whose lingering step and disappointed air spoke to his heart the rejection of his suit. He told the Count that Mary did not at present feel for him those sentiments of affection which would justify her in accepting his proposals. This information, though it shocked the hopes of the Count, did not entirely destroy them; for he yet believed that time and assiduity might befriend his wishes. While these Noblemen were leaning on the walls of the castle, engaged in earnest conversation, they observed on a distant hill a cloud emerging from the verge of the horizon, whose dusky hue glittered with sudden light; in an instant they descried the glance of arms, and a troop of armed men poured in long succession over the hill, and hurried down its side to the plains below. The Earl thought he recognized the clan of the Baron.* It was the Baron himself who now advanced at the head of his people, in search of that revenge which had been hitherto denied him; and who, determined on conquest, had brought with him an host which he thought more than sufficient to overwhelm the castle of his enemy.

The messenger, who had been sent with the challenge, had been detained a prisoner by Malcolm; who in the mean time had hastened his preparations to surprize the castle of Athlin. The detention of his servant had awakened the suspicions of the Earl, and he had taken precautions to guard against the designs of his enemy. He had summoned his clan to hold themselves in readiness for a sudden attack, and had prepared his castle for the worst emergency. He now sent a messenger to the clan with such orders as he judged expedient, arranged his plans within the walls, and took his station on the ramparts to observe the movements of his enemy. The Count, clad in arms, stood by his side. Alleyn was posted with a party within the great gate of the castle.

The Baron advanced with his people, and quickly surrounded

the walls. Within all was silent; the castle seemed to repose in security; and the Baron, certain of victory, congratulated himself on the success of the enterprize, when observing the Earl, whose person was concealed in armour, he called to him to surrender himself and his Chief to the arms of Malcolm. The Earl answered the summons with an arrow from his bow,* which, missing the Baron, pierced one of his attendants. The archers, who had been planted behind the walls, now discovered themselves, and discharged a shower of arrows; at the same time every part of the castle appeared thronged with the soldiers of the Earl, who hurled on the heads of the astonished besiegers, lances and other missile weapons with unceasing rapidity. The alarum bell now rung out the signal to that part of the clan without the walls, and they immediately poured upon the enemy, who, confounded by this unexpected attack, had scarcely time to defend themselves. The clang of arms resounded through the air, with the shouts of the victors, and the groans of the dying. The fear of the Baron, which had principally operated on the minds of his people, was now overcome by surprize, and the fear of death; and on the first repulse, they deserted from the ranks in great numbers, and fled to the distant hills. In vain the Baron endeavoured to rally his soldiers, and keep them to the charge; they yielded to a stronger impulse than the menaces of their Chief, who was now left with less than half his numbers at the foot of the walls. The Baron, to whom cowardice was unknown, disdaining to retreat, continued the attack. At length the gates of the castle were thrown open, and a party issued upon the assailants, headed by the Earl and the Count, who divided in quest of Malcolm. The Count fought in vain, and the search of Osbert was equally fruitless; their adversary was no where to be found. Osbert, apprehensive of his gaining admittance to the castle by stratagem, was returning in haste to the gates, when he received the stroke of a sword upon his shoulder; his armour had broke the force of the blow, and the wound it had given was slight. He turned his sword, and facing his enemy, discovered a soldier of Malcolm's who attacked him with a desperate courage. The encounter was furious and long; dexterity and equal valour seemed to animate both the combatants.

Alleyn, who observed from his post the danger of the Earl, flew instantly to his assistance; but the crisis of the scene was past ere he arrived; the weapon of Osbert had pierced the side of his adversary, and he fell to the ground. The Earl disarmed him, and holding over him his sword, bade him ask his life. 'I have no life to ask,' said Malcolm, whose fainting voice the Earl now discovered, 'if I had, 'tis death only I would accept from you. O! cursed—.' He would have finished the sentence, but his wound flowed apace, and he fainted with loss of blood. The Earl threw down his sword, and calling a party of his people, he committed to them the care of the Baron, and ordered them to proceed and seize the castle of Dunbayne. Understanding their Chief was mortally wounded, the remains of Malcolm's army had fled from the walls. The people of the Earl proceeded without interruption, and took possession of the castle without opposition.

The wounds of the Baron were examined when he reached Dunbayne, and a dubious sentence of the event was pronounced. His countenance marked the powerful workings of his mind, which seemed labouring with an unknown evil; he threw his eyes eagerly round the apartment, as if in search of some object which was not present. After several attempts to speak, 'Flatter me not,' said he, 'with hopes of life; it is flitting fast away; but while I have breath to speak, let me see the Baroness.' She came, and hanging over his couch in silent horror, received his words: 'I have injured you, Madam, I fear beyond reparation. In these last few moments let me endeavour to relieve my conscience by discovering to you my guilt and my remorse.' The Baroness started, fearful of the coming sentence. 'You had a son.' 'What of my son?' 'You had a son, whom my boundless ambition doomed to exile from his parents and his heritage, and who I caused you to believe died in your absence.' 'Where is my child!' exclaimed the Baroness. 'I know not,' resumed Malcolm, 'I committed him to the care of a man and woman who then lived on a remote part of my lands, but a few years after they disappeared, and I have never heard of them since. The boy passed for a foundling whom I had saved from perishing. One servant only I entrusted with the secret; the rest were imposed upon. Thus far I tell you, Madam, to prompt you to enquiry, and to assuage the agonies of a bleeding conscience. I have other deeds—' The Baroness could hear no more; she was carried insensible from the apartment. Laura, shocked at her condition, was informed of its cause, and filial tenderness watched over her with unwearied attention.

In the mean time the Earl, on quitting Malcolm, had returned immediately to the castle, and was the first messenger of that event which would probably avenge the memory of his father, and terminate the distresses of his family. The sight of Osbert, and the news he brought, revived the Countess and Mary, who had retired during the assault into an inner apartment of the castle for greater security, and who had suffered, during that period, all the terrors which their situation could inspire. They were soon after joined by the Count and by Alleyn, whose conduct did not pass unnoticed by the Earl. The cheek of Mary glowed at the relation of this new instance of his worth; and it was Alleyn's sweet reward to observe her emotion. There was a sentiment in the heart of Osbert which struggled against the pride of birth; he wished to reward the services and the noble spirit of the youth, with the virtues of Mary; but the authority of early prejudice silenced the grateful impulse, and swept from his heart the characters of truth.

The Earl, accompanied by the Count, now hastened to the castle of Dunbayne, to cheer the Baroness and her daughter with their presence. As they approached the castle, the stillness and desolation of the scene bespoke the situation of its lord; his people were entirely dispersed, a few only of his centinels wandered before the eastern gate; who, having made no opposition, were suffered by the Earl's people to remain. Few of the Baron's people were to be seen; those few were unarmed, and appeared the effigies of fallen greatness. As the Earl crossed the platform, the remembrance of the past crowded upon his mind. The agonies which he had there suffered,—the image of death which glared upon his sight, aggravated by the bitter and ignominious circumstances which attended his fate; the figure of Malcolm, mighty in injustice, and cruel in power; whose countenance, smiling horribly in triumphant revenge, sent to his heart the stroke of anguish;—each circumstance of torture arose to his imagination in the glowing colours of truth; he shuddered as he passed; and the contrast of the present scene touched his heart with the most affecting sentiments. He saw the innate and active power of justice, which pervades all the circumstances even of this life like vital principle, and shines through the obscurity of human actions to the virtuous, the pure ray of Heaven;—to the guilty, the destructive glare of lightning.

On enquiring for the Baroness, they were told she was in the apartment of Malcolm, whose moment of dissolution was now approaching. The name of the Count was delivered to the Baroness, and overheard by the Baron, who desired to see him. Louisa went out to receive her noble relation with all the joy which a meeting so desirable and so unlooked for, could inspire. On seeing Osbert, her tears flowed fast, and she thanked him for his generous care, in a manner that declared a deep sense of his services. Leaving him, she conducted the Count to Malcolm, who lay on his couch surrounded with the stillness and horrors of death. He raised his languid head, and discovered a countenance wild and terrific, whose ghastly aspect was overspread with the paleness of death. The beauteous Laura, overcome by the scene, hung like a drooping lily over his couch, dropping fast her tears. 'My lord,' said Malcolm, in a low tone, 'you see before you a wretch, anxious to relieve the agony of a guilty mind. My vices have destroyed the peace of this lady,—have robbed her of a son—but she will disclose to you the secret guilt, which I have now no time to tell. I have for some years received, as you now well know, the income of those foreign lands which are her due; as a small reparation for the injuries she has sustained, I bequeath to her all the possessions which I lawfully inherit, and resign her into your protection. To ask oblivion of the past of you, Madam, and of you, my Lord, is what I dare not do; yet it would be some consolation to my departing spirit, to be assured of your forgiveness.' The Baroness was too much affected to reply but by a look of assent; the Count assured him of forgiveness, and besought him to compose his mind for his approaching fate. 'Composure, my Lord, is not for me; my Life has been marked with vice, and my death with the bitterness of fruitless remorse. I have understood virtue, but I have loved vice. I do not now lament that I am punished, but that I have deserved punishment.' The Baron sunk on his couch, and in a few moments after expired in a strong sigh. Thus terminated the life of a man, whose understanding might have reached the happiness of virtue, but whose actions displayed the features of vice.*

From this melancholy scene, the Baroness, with the Count and Laura, retired to her apartment, where the Earl awaited their return with anxious solicitude. The sternness of justice for a moment relaxed when he heard of Malcolm's death; his heart would have sighed with compassion, had not the remembrance of his father crossed his mind, and checked the impulse. 'I can now, Madam,' said he, addressing the Baroness, 'restore you a part of those possessions which were once your Lord's, and which ought to have been the inheritance of your son; this castle from henceforth is yours; I resign it to its lawful owner.' The Baroness was overcome with the remembrance of his services, and could scarcely thank him but with her tears. The servant whom the Baron had mentioned as the confidant of his iniquities, was sent for, and interrogated concerning the infant he had charge of. From him, however, little comfort was received; for he could only tell that he had conveyed the child, by the orders of his master, to a cottage on the furthest borders of his estates, where he had delivered it to the care of a woman, who there lived with her husband. These people received at the same time a sum of money for its support, with a promise of future supplies. For some years he had been punctual in the payment of the sums entrusted to him by the Baron, but at length he yielded to the temptation of withholding them for his own use; and on enquiring for the people some years after, he found they were gone from the place. The conditions of the Baroness's pardon to the man depended on his endeavours to repair the injury he had promoted, by a strict search for the people to whom he had committed her child. She now consulted with her friends on the best means to be pursued in this business, and immediately sent off messengers to different parts of the country to gather information.

The Baroness was now released from oppression and imprisonment; she was reinstated in her ancient possessions, to which were added all the hereditary lands of Malcolm, together with his personal fortune: she was surrounded by those whom she most loved, and in the midst of a people who loved her; yet the consequence of the Baron's guilt had left in her heart one drop of gall which embittered each source of happiness, and made her life melancholy and painful.

The Count was now her visitor; she was much consoled by his presence; and Laura's hours were often enlivened by the conversation of the Earl, to whom her heart was tenderly attached, and whose frequent visits to the castle were devoted to love and her.

The felicity of Matilda now appeared as perfect and as permanent as is consistent with the nature of sublunary* beings. Justice was done to the memory of her Lord, and her beloved son was spared to bless the evening of her days. The father of Laura had ever been friendly to the house of Athlin, and her delicacy felt no repugnance to the union which Osbert solicited. But her happiness, whatever it might appear, was incomplete; she saw the settled melancholy of Mary, for love still corroded her heart and notwithstanding her efforts, shaded her countenance. The Countess wished to produce those nuptials with the Count which she thought would re-establish the peace of her child, and insure her future felicity. She omitted no opportunity of pressing his suit, which she managed with a delicacy that rendered it less painful to Mary; whose words, however, were few in reply, and who could seldom bear that the subject should ever be long continued. Her settled aversion to the addresses of the Count, at length baffled the expectations of Matilda, and shewed her the fallacy of her efforts. She thought it improper to suffer the Count any longer to nourish in his heart a vain hope; and she reluctantly commissioned the Earl to undeceive him on this point.

With the Baroness, month after month still elapsed in fruitless search of her son; the people with whom he had been placed were no where to be found, and no track was discovered which might lead to the truth. The distress of the Baroness can only be imagined; she resigned herself, in calm despair, to mourn in silence the easy confidence which had entrusted her child to the care of those who had betrayed him. Though happiness was denied her, she was unwilling to with-hold it from those whom it awaited; and at length yielded to the entreaties of the Earl, and became its advocate with Laura, for the nuptials which were to unite their fate.

The Earl introduced the Countess and Mary to the castle of Dunbayne. Similarity of sentiment and disposition united Matilda and the Baroness in a lasting friendship. Mary and Laura were not less pleased with each other. The dejection of the Count at sight of Mary, declared the ardor of his passion, and would have awakened in her breast something more than compassion, had not her heart been pre-occupied. Alleyn, who could think of Mary only, wandered through the castle of Athlin a solitary being, who fondly haunts the spot where his happiness lies buried. His prudence formed resolutions, which his passion as quickly broke; and cheated by love, though followed by despair, he delayed his departure from day to day, and the illusion of yesterday continued to be the illusion of the morrow. The Earl, attached to his virtues, and grateful for his services, would have bestowed on him every honour but that alone which could give him happiness, and which his pride would have suffered him to accept. Yet the honours which he refused—he refused with a grace so modest, as to conciliate kindness rather than wound generosity.

In a gallery on the North side of the castle, which was filled with pictures of the family, hung a portrait of Mary. She was drawn in the dress which she wore on the day of the festival, when she was led by the Earl into the hall, and presented as the partner of Alleyn. The likeness was striking, and expressive of all the winning grace of the original. As often as Alleyn could steal from observation, be retired to this gallery, to contemplate the portrait of her who was ever present to his imagination: here he could breath that sigh which her presence restrained, and shed those tears which her presence forbade to flow. As he stood one day in this place wrapt in melancholy musing, his ear was struck with the notes of sweet music; they seemed to issue from the bottom of the gallery. The instrument was touched with an exquisite expression, and in a voice whose tones floated on the air in soft undulations, he distinguished the following words, which he remembered to be an ode composed by the Earl, and presented to Mary, who had set it to music the day before.

MORNING*

Darkness! through thy chilling glooms,
  Weakly trembles twilight grey;
Twilight fades—and Morning comes,
  And melts thy shadows swift away!

She comes in her ætherial car,
  Involv'd in many a varying hue;
And thro' the azure shoots afar,
  Spirit—light—and life anew!

Her breath revives the drooping flowers,
  Her ray dissolves the dews of night;
Recalls the sprightly-moving hours.
  And the green scene unveils in light!

Her's the fresh gale that wanders wild
  O'er mountain top, and dewy glade;
And fondly steals the breath, beguil'd,
  Of ev'ry flow'r in every shade.

Mother of Roses—bright Aurora!*—hail!
  Thee shall the chorus of the hours salute,
And song of early birds from ev'ry vale,
  And blithsome* horn, and fragrant zephyr mute!

And oft as rising o'er the plain,
  Thou and thy roseate Nymphs appear,
This simple song in choral strain,
  From rapturing Bards* shall meet thine ear.

CHORUS

Dance ye lightly—lightly on!
  'Tis the bold lark thro' the air,
Hails your beauties with his song;
  Lightly—lightly fleeting fair!

Entranced in the sweet sounds, he had proceeded some steps down the gallery, when the music ceased. He stopped. After a short pause it returned, and as he advanced he distinguished these words, sung in a low voice mournfully sweet:

In solitude I mourn thy reign,
Ah! youth belov'd—but lov'd in vain!

The voice was broken and lost in sobs; the chords of the lute were wildly struck: and in a few moments silence ensued. He stepped on towards the spot whence the sounds had proceeded, and through a door which was left open, he discovered Mary hanging over her lute dissolved in tears. He stood for some moments absorbed in mute admiration, and unobserved by Mary, who was lost in her tears, till a sigh which escaped him, recalled her to reality; she raised her eyes, and beheld the object of her secret sorrows. She arose in confusion; the blush on her cheek betrayed her heart; she was retiring in haste from Alleyn, who remained at the entrance of the room the statue of despair, when she was intercepted by the Earl, who entered by the door she was opening; her eyes were red with weeping; he glanced on her a look of surprize and displeasure, and passed on to the gallery followed by Alleyn, who was now awakened from his trance. 'From you Alleyn,' said the Earl, in a tone of displeasure, 'I expected other conduct; on your word I relied, and your word has deceived me.' 'Hear me, my Lord,' returned the youth, 'your confidence I have never abused; hear me.' 'I have now no time for parley,' replied Osbert, 'my moments are precious; some future hour of leisure may suffice.' So saying, he walked away with an abrupt haughtiness, which touched the soul of Alleyn, who disdained to pursue him with further explanation. He was now completely wretched. The same accident which had unveiled to him the heart of Mary, and the full extent of that happiness which fate with-held, confirmed him in despair. The same accident had exposed the delicacy of her he loved to a cruel shock, and had subjected his honour to suspicion; and to a severe rebuke from him, by whom it was his pride to be respected, and for whose safety he had suffered imprisonment, and encountered death.

Mary had quitted the closet distressed and perplexed. She perceived the mistake of the Earl, and it shocked her. She wished to undeceive him; but he was gone to the castle of Dunbayne, to pay one of those visits which were soon to conclude in the nuptials, and whence he did not return till evening. The scene which he had witnessed in the morning, involved him in tumult of distress. He considered the mutual passion which filled the bosom of his sister and Alleyn; he had surprized them in a solitary apartment; he had observed the tender and melancholy air of Alleyn, and the tears and confusion of Mary; and he at first did not hesitate to believe that the interview had been appointed. In the heat of his displeasure he had rejected the explanation of Alleyn with a haughty resentment, which the late scene alone could have excited, and which the delusion it had occasioned alone could excuse. Cooler consideration however, brought to his mind the delicacy and the amiable pride of Mary, and the integrity of Alleyn; and he accused himself of a too hasty decision. The zealous services of Alleyn came to his heart; he repented that he had treated him so rigorously; and on his return enquired for him, that he might hear an explanation, and that he might soften the asperity of his former behaviour.

CHAPTER XI

ALLEYN was no where to be found. The Earl went himself in quest of him, but without success. As he returned from the terrace, chagrined and disappointed, he observed two persons cross the platform at some distance before him; and he could perceive by the dim moon-light which fell upon the spot, that they were not of the castle. He called to them: no answer was returned; but at the sound of his voice they quickened their pace, and almost instantly disappeared in the darkness of the ramparts. Surprised at this phœnomenon, the Earl followed with hasty steps, and endeavoured to pursue the way they had taken. He walked on silently, but there was no sound to direct his steps. When he came to the extremity of the rampart, which formed the North angle of the castle, he stopped to examine the spot, and to listen if any thing was stirring. No person was to be seen, and all was hushed. After he had stood some time survey-ing the rampart, he heard the low restrained voice of a person unknown, but the distance prevented his distinguishing the sub-ject of the conversation. The voice seemed to approach the place where he stood. He drew his sword, and watched in silence their motions. They continued to advance, till, suddenly stopping, they turned, and took a long survey of the fabric. Their dis-course was conducted in a low tone; but the Earl could discover by the vehemence of their gesture, and the caution of their steps, that they were upon some design dangerous to the peace of the castle. Having finished their examination, they turned again towards the place where the Earl still remained; the shade of a high turret concealed him from their view, and they con-tinued to approach till they arrived within a short space of him, when they turned through a ruined arch-way of the castle, and were lost in the dark recesses of the pile. Astonished at what he had seen, Osbert hastened to the castle, whence he dispatched some of his people in search of the unknown fugitives; he ac-companied some of his domestics to the spot where they had last disappeared. They entered the arch-way, which led to a decayed part of the castle; they followed over broken pavement the remains of a passage, which was closed by a low obscure door almost concealed from sight by the thick ivy which overshadowed it. On opening this door, they descended a flight of steps which led under the castle, so extremely narrow and broken as to make the descent both difficult and dangerous. The powerful damps of long pent-up vapours extinguished their light, and the Earl and his attendants were compelled to remain in utter darkness, while one of them went round to the habitable part of the castle to relume* the lamp. While they awaited in silence the return of light, a short breathing was distinctly heard at intervals, near the place where they stood. The servants shook with fear, and the Earl was not wholly unmoved. They remained entirely silent, listening its return, when a sound of footsteps slowly stealing through the vault, startled them. The Earl demanded who passed;—he was answered only by the deep echoes of his voice. They clashed their swords and had advanced, when the steps hastily retired before them. The Earl rushed forward, pursuing the sound, till overtaking the person who fled, he seized him; a short scuffle ensued; the strength of Osbert was too powerful for his antagonist, who was nearly overcome, when the point of a sword from an unknown hand pierced his side, he relinquished his grasp, and fell to the ground. His domestics, whom the activity of their master had outran, now came up; but the assassins, whoever they were, had accomplished their escape, for the sound of their steps was quickly lost in the distance of the vaults. They endeavoured to raise the Earl, who lay speechless on the ground; but they knew not how to convey him from that place of horror, for they were yet in total darkness, and unacquainted with the place. In this situation, every moment of delay seemed an age. Some of them tried to find their way to the entrance, but their efforts were defeated by the darkness, and the ruinous situation of the place. The light at length appeared, and discovered the Earl insensible, and weltering in his blood. He was conveyed into the castle, where the horror of the Countess on seeing him borne into the hall, may be easily imagined. By the help of proper applications he was restored to life; his wound was examined, and found to be dangerous; he was carried to bed in a state which gave very faint hopes of recovery. The astonishment of the Countess, on hearing the adventure, was equalled only by her distress. All her conjectures concerning the designs, and the identity of the assassin, were vague and uncertain. She knew not on whom to fix the stigma; nor could discover any means by which to penetrate this mysterious affair. The people who had remained in the vaults to pursue the search, now returned to Matilda. Every recess of the castle, and every part of the ramparts, had been explored, yet no one could be found; and the mystery of the proceeding was heightened by the manner in which the men had effected their escape.

Mary watched over her brother in silent anguish, yet she strove to conceal her distress, that she might encourage the Countess to hope. The Countess endeavoured to resign herself to the event with a kind of desperate fortitude. There is a certain point of misery, beyond which the mind becomes callous, and acquires a sort of artificial calm. Excess of misery may be said to blast the vital powers of feeling, and by a natural consequence consumes its own principle. Thus it was with Matilda; a long succession of trials had reduced her to a state of horrid tranquillity, which followed the first shock of the present event. It was not so with Laura; young in misfortune, and gay in hope, she saw happiness fade from her grasp, with a warmth of feeling untouched by the chill of disappointment. When the news of the Earl's situation reached her, she was overcome with affliction, and pined in silent anguish. The Count hastened to Osbert, but grief sat heavy at his heart, and he had no power to offer to others the comfort which he wanted himself.

A fever, which was the consequence of his wounds, added to the danger of the Earl, and to the despair of his family. During this period, Alleyn had not been seen at the castle; and his absence at this time, raised in Mary a variety of distressing apprehensions. Osbert enquired for him, and wished to see him. The servant who had been sent to his father's cottage, brought word that it was some days since he had been there, and that nobody knew whither he was gone. The surprize was universal; but the effect it produced was various and opposite. A collection of strange and concomitant circumstances, now forced a suspicion on the mind of the Countess, which her heart, and the remembrance of the former conduct of Alleyn, at once condemned. She had heard of what passed between the Earl and him in the gallery; his immediate absence, the event which followed, and his subsequent flight, formed a chain of evidence which compelled her, with the utmost reluctance, to believe him concerned in the affair which had once more involved her house in misery. Mary had too much confidence in her knowledge of his character, to admit a suspicion of this nature. She rejected, with instant disdain, the idea of uniting Alleyn with dishonour; and that he should be guilty of an action so base as the present, soared beyond all the bounds of possibility. Yet she felt a strange solicitude concerning him, and apprehension for his safety tormented her incessantly. The anguish in which he had quitted the apartment, her brother's injurious treatment, and his consequent absence, all conspired to make her fear that despair had driven him to commit some act of violence on himself.

The Earl, in the delirium of the fever, raved continually of Laura and of Alleyn; they were the sole subjects of his ramblings. Seizing one day the hand of Mary, who sat mournfully by his bed-side, and looking for some time pensively in her face, 'weep not, my Laura,' said he, 'Malcolm, nor all the powers on earth shall tear you from me; his walls—his guards—what are they? I'll wrest you from his hold, or perish. I have a friend whose valour will do much for us;—a friend—O! name him not; these are strange times; beware of trusting. I could have given him my very life—but not—I will not name him.' Then starting to the other side of the bed, and looking earnestly towards the door with an expression of sorrow not to be described, 'not all the miseries which my worst enemy has heaped upon me; not all the horrors of imprisonment and death, have ever touched my soul with a sting so sharp as thy unfaithfulness.' Mary was so much shocked by this scene, that she left the room and retired to her own apartment to indulge the agony of grief it occasioned.

The situation of the Earl grew daily more alarming; and the fever, which had not yet reached its crisis, kept the hopes and fears of his family suspended. In one of his lucid intervals, addressing himself to the Countess in the most pathetic manner, he requested, that as death might probably soon separate him for ever from her he most loved, he might see Laura once again before he died. She came, and weeping over him, a scene of anguish ensued too poignant for description. He gave her his last vows; she took of him a last look; and with a breaking heart tearing herself away, was carried to Dunbayne in a state of danger little inferior to his.

The agitation he had suffered during this interview, caused a return of phrenzy more violent than any fit he had yet suffered; exhausted by it, he at length sunk into a sleep, which continued without interruption for near four and twenty hours. During this time his repose was quiet and profound, and afforded the Countess and Mary, who watched him alternately, the consolations of hope. When he awoke he was perfectly sensible, and in a very altered state from that he had been in a few hours before. The crisis of the disorder was now past, and from that time it rapidly declined till he was restored to perfect health.

The joy of Laura, whose health gradually returned with returning peace, and that of his family, was such as the merits of the Earl deserved. This joy, however, suffered a short interruption from the Count of Santmorin, who, entering one morning the apartment of the Baroness, with letters in his hand, came to acquaint her that he had just received news of the death of a distant relation, who had bequeathed him some estates of value, to which it was necessary he should immediately lay claim; and that he was, therefore, obliged, however reluctantly, to set off for Switzerland without delay. Though the Baroness rejoiced with all his friends, at his good fortune, she regretted, with them, the necessity of his abrupt departure. He took leave of them, and particularly of Mary, for whom his passion was still the same, with much emotion; and it was some time ere the space he had left in their society was filled up, and ere they resumed their wonted cheerfulness.

Preparations were now making for the approaching nuptials, and the day of their celebration was at length fixed. The ceremony was to be performed in a chapel belonging to the castle of Dunbayne, by the chaplain of the Baroness. Mary only was to attend as bride-maid; and the Countess also, with the Baroness, was to be present. The absence of the Count was universally regretted; for from his hand the Earl was to have received his bride. The office was now to be supplied by a neighbouring Laird, whom the family of the Baroness had long esteemed. At the earnest request of Laura, Mary consented to spend the night preceding the day of marriage, at the castle of Dunbayne. The day so long and so anxiously expected by the Earl at length arrived. The morning was extremely fine, and the joy which glowed in his heart seemed to give additional splendor to the scene around him. He set off, accompanied by the Countess, for the castle of Dunbayne. He anticipated the joy with which he should soon retrace the way he then travelled, with Laura by his side, whom death alone could then separate from him. On their arrival they were received by the Baroness, who enquired for Mary; and the Countess and Osbert were thrown into the utmost consternation, when they learned that she had not been seen at the castle. The nuptials were again deferred; the castle was a scene of universal confusion. The Earl returned home instantly to dispatch his people in search of Mary. On enquiry, he learned that the servants who had attended her, had not been heard of since their departure with their lady. Still more alarmed by this intelligence he rode himself in pursuit, yet not knowing which course to take. Several days were employed in a fruitless search; no footstep of her flight could be traced.

CHAPTER XII

MARY, in the mean time, suffered all the terror which her situation could excite. On her way to Dunbayne, she had been overtaken by a party of armed men, who seized her bridle, and after engaging her servants in a feigned resistance, carried her off senseless. On recovering, she found herself travelling through a forest, whose glooms were deepened by the shades of night. The moon, which was now up, glancing through the trees, served to shew the dreary aspect of the place, and the number of men who surrounded her; and she was seized with a terror that almost deprived her of reason. They travelled all night, during which a profound silence was observed. At the dawn of day she found herself on the skirts of a heath, to whose wide desolation her eye could discover no limits. Before they entered on the waste, they halted at the entrance of a cave, formed in a rock, which was overhung with pine and fir; where, spreading their breakfast on the grass, they offered refreshments to Mary, whose mind was too much distracted to suffer her to partake of them. She implored them in the most moving accents, to tell her from whom they came, and whither they were carrying her; but they were insensible to her tears and her entreaties, and she was compelled to await, in silent terror, the extremity of her fate. They pursued their journey over the wilds, and towards the close of day approached the ruins of an abbey, whose broken arches and lonely towers arose in gloomy grandeur through the obscurity of evening.* It stood the solitary inhabitant of the waste,—a monument of mortality and of ancient superstition, and the frowning majesty of its aspect seemed to command silence and veneration. The chilly dews fell thick, and Mary, fatigued in body, and harassed in mind, lay almost expiring on her horse, when they stopped under an arch of the ruin. She was not so ill as to be insensible to the objects around her; the awful solitude of the place, and the solemn aspect of the fabric, whose effect was heightened by the falling glooms of evening, chilled her heart with horror; and when they took her from the horse, she shrieked in the agonies of a last despair. They bore her over loose stones to a part of the building, which had been formerly the cloisters of the abbey, but which was now fallen to decay, and overgrown with ivy. There was, however, at the extremity of these cloisters a nook, which had withstood with hardier strength the ravages of time; the roof was here entire, and the shattered stanchions of the casements still remained. Hither they carried Mary, and laid her almost lifeless on the grassy pavement, while some of the ruffians hastened to light a fire of the heath and sticks they could pick up. They took out their provisions, and placed themselves round the fire, where they had not long been seated, when the sound of distant thunder foretold an approaching storm. A violent storm, accompanied with peals which shook the pile, came on. They were sheltered from the heaviness of the rain; but the long and vivid flashes of lightning which glanced through the casements, alarmed them all. The shrieks of Mary were loud and continued; and the fears of the ruffians did not prevent their uttering dreadful imprecations at her distress. One of them, in the fury of his resentment, swore she should be gagged; and seizing her resistless hands to execute the purpose, her cries redoubled. The servants who had betrayed her, were not yet so entirely lost to the feelings of humanity, as to stand regardless of her present distress; though they could not resist the temptations of a bribe, they were unwilling their lady should be loaded with unnecessary misery. They opposed the ruffians; a dispute ensued; and the violence of the contest arose so high, that they determined to fight for the decision. Amid the peals of thunder, the oaths and execrations of the combatants, added terror to the scene. The strength of the ruffians were superior to that of their opponents; and Mary, beholding victory deciding against herself, uttered a loud scream, when the attention of the whole party was surprized by the sound of a footstep in the cloister. Immediately after a man rushed into the place, and drawing his sword, demanded the cause of the tumult. Mary, who lay almost expiring on the ground, now raised her eyes; but what were her sensations, when she raised them to Alleyn!—who now stood before her petrified with horror. Before he could fly to her assistance, the attacks of the ruffians obliged him to defend himself; he parried their blows for some time, but he must inevitably have yielded to the force of numbers, had not the trampling of feet, which fast approached, called off for a moment their attention. In an instant the place was filled with men. The astonishment of Alleyn was, if possible, now encreased; for the Earl, followed by a party, now entered. The Earl, when he perceived Alleyn, stood at the entrance, aghast.—But resuming his firmness, he bade him defend himself. The loud voice of Osbert re-called Mary, and observing their menacing attitudes, she collected just strength sufficient to throw herself between them. Alleyn dropped his sword, and raised her from the ground; when the Earl rudely pushed him away, and snatched her to his heart. 'Hear me, Osbert,' was all she could say. 'Declare who brought her hither,' said the Earl sternly to Alleyn. 'I know not,' replied he, 'you must ask those men whom your people have secured. If my life is hateful to you, strike! and spare me the anguish of defending it against the brother of Mary.' The Earl hesitated in surprize, and the generosity of Alleyn called a blush into his face. He was going to have replied, but was interrupted by some of his men, who had been engaged in a sharp contest with the ruffians, two of whom they had secured, and now brought to their lord; the rest were fled. In the person of one of them, the Earl discovered his own servant, who sinking in his presence with conscious guilt, fell on his knees imploring mercy. 'Wretch,' said the Earl, seizing him, and holding his sword over his head, 'declare by whose authority you have acted, and all you know of the affair;—remember your life depends on the truth of your assertions.' 'I'll tell the truth, my Lord,' replied the trembling wretch, 'and nothing else as I hope for mercy. About three weeks ago,— no, it is not so much; about a fortnight ago, when I was sent on a message to the lady Malcolm, the Count de Santmorin's gentleman—' 'The Count de Santmorin!' re-echoed the whole company. 'But proceed,' said Osbert. 'The Count de Santmorin's gentleman called me into a private room, where he told me to wait for his master, who would soon be there.' 'Be quick,' said the Earl, 'proceed to facts.' 'I will, my lord; the Count came, and said to me, "Robert, I have observed you, and I think you can be faithful," he said so, my lord,—God forgive me!' 'Well—well, proceed.' 'Where was I?'—'Oh! he said, "I think you can be faithful."'—'Good God! this is beyond endurance; you trifle, rascal, with my patience, to give your associates time for escape; be brief, or you die.' 'I will, my lord, as I hope for life. He took from his pocket a handful of gold, which he gave me; —"can you be secret, Robert?" said he,—"yes, my lord Count," said I, God forgive me!—"Then observe what I say to you. You often attend your young lady in her rides to Dunbayne."'—'What, then it was the Count de Santmorin who commissioned you to undertake this scheme!' 'Not me only, my lord.' 'Answer my question; was the Count the author of this plot?' 'He was, my lord.' 'And where is he?' said Osbert, in a stern voice. 'I know not, as I am a living creature. He embarked, as you know, my lord, not far from the castle of Dunbayne, and we were travelling to a distant part of the coast to meet him, when we were all to have set sail for Switzerland.' 'You cannot be ignorant of the place of your destination,' said the Earl, turning to the other prisoner; 'where is your employer?' 'That is not for me to tell,' said he, in a sullen tone. 'Reveal the truth,' said the Earl, turning towards him the point of his sword, 'or we will find a way to make you.' 'The place where we were to meet the Count, had no name.' 'You know the way to it.' 'I do.' 'Then lead me thither.' 'Never!'—'Never! Your life shall answer the refusal,' said Osbert, pointing the sword to his breast. 'Strike!' said the Count, throwing off the cloak which had concealed him; 'strike! and rid me of a being which passion has made hateful to me;—strike!—and make the first moment of my entering this place, the last of my guilt.' A faint scream was uttered by Mary; the small remains of her strength forsook her, and she sunk on the pavement. The Earl started a few steps back, and stood suspended in wonder. The looks of the whole group 'efy description. 'Take a sword,' said the Earl, recovering himself, 'and defend your life.' 'Never, my lord, never! Though I have been hurried by the force of passion to rob you of a sister, I will not aggravate my guilt by the murder of the brother. Your life has already been once endangered through my means, though not by my design; Heaven knows the anguish which that accident cost me. The impetuosity of passion impelled me onward with irresistible fury; it urged me to violate the sacred duties of gratitude, of friendship—and of humanity. To live in shame, and in the consciousness of guilt, is a living death. With your sword do justice to yourself and virtue; and spare me the misery of long comparing what I am, with what I was.' 'Away, you trifle,' said the Earl, 'defend yourself.' The Count repeated his refusal. 'And you, villain,' said Osbert, turning to the man who had confessed the plot, 'you pretended ignorance of the presence of the Count; your perfidy shall be rewarded.' 'As I now plead for mercy, my lord, I knew not he was here.' 'The fellow speaks truth,' said the Count, 'he was ignorant of the place where he was to meet me. I was approaching this spot to discover myself to the dear object of my passion, when your people surprised and took me.' Mary confirmed the testimony of the Count, by declaring that she had not till that moment seen him since she quitted the castle of Dunbayne. She pleaded for his life, and also for the servants, who had opposed the cruelty of their comrades. 'I am no assassin,' said the Earl, 'let the Count take a sword, and fight me on equal terms.'—'Shall virtue be reduced to an equality with vice?' said the Count, 'No, my lord,—plunge your sword in my heart, and expiate my guilt.' The Earl still urged him to defence; and the Count still persisted in refusal. Touched by the recollection of past friendship, and grieved that a soul like the Count's should ever be under the dominion of vice, Osbert threw down his sword, and, overcome with a sort of tenderness—'Go, my lord, your person is safe; and if it is necessary to your peace,— stretching forth his hand,—take my forgiveness.' The Count, overcome by his generosity, and by a sense of his own unworthiness, shrunk back: 'Forbear, my lord, to wound by your goodness, a mind already too sensible of its own debasement; nor excite, by your generosity, a remorse too keen to be endured. Your reproaches I can bear,—your vengeance I solicit,—but your kindness inflicts a torture too exquisite for my soul.' 'Never, my lord,' continued he, the big tear swelling in his eye,—'never more shall your friendship be polluted by my unworthiness. Since you will not satisfy justice, by taking my life, I go to lose it in the obscurity of distant regions. Yet, ere I go, suffer me to make one last request to you, and to that dear lady whom I have thus injured, and on whom my eyes now gaze for the last time,—suffer me to hope that you will blot from your memory the existence of Santmorin.' He concluded the sentence with a groan, which vibrated upon the hearts of all present; and without waiting for a reply, hurried from the scene. The Earl had turned away his head in pity, and when he again looked round to reply, perceived that the Count was departed; he followed his steps through the cloister,—he called—but he was gone.

Alleyn had observed the Count with a mixture of pity and admiration; and he sighed for the weakness of human nature. 'How,' said the Earl, returning eagerly to Alleyn,—'how can I recompense you for my injurious suspicions, and my injurious treatment?—How can you forgive, or I forget, my injustice? But the mystery of this affair, and the doubtful appearance of circumstances, must speak for me.' 'O! let us talk no more of this, my lord,' replied Alleyn, with emotion; 'let us only rejoice at the safety of our dear lady, and offer her the comfort she is so much in want of.' The fire was re-kindled, and the Earl's servants laid before him some wine, and other provisions. Mary, who had not tasted any food since she left the castle, now took some wine; it revived her, and enabled her to take other nourishment. She enquired, what happy circumstance had enabled the Earl to trace her route. 'Ever since I discovered your flight,' said he, 'I have been in pursuit of you. Chance directed me over these wilds, when I was driven by the storm to seek shelter among these ruins. The light, and an uproar of voices, drew me to the cloister, where, to my unutterable astonishment, I discovered you and Alleyn: Spare me the remembrance of what followed.' Mary wished to enquire what brought Alleyn to the place; but delicacy kept her silent. Osbert, however, whose anxiety for his sister had hitherto allowed him to attend only to her, now relieved her from the pain of lengthened suspense. 'By what strange accident was you brought hither?' said he to Alleyn, 'and what motive has induced you so long to absent yourself from the castle?' At the last question, Alleyn blushed, and an involuntary sigh escaped him. Mary understood the blush and the sigh, and awaited his reply in trembling emotion. 'I fled, my lord, from

your displeasure, and to tear myself from an object too dangerous, alas! for my peace. I sought to wear away in absence, a
passion which must ever be hopeless, but which, I now perceive,
is interwoven with my existence.—But forgive, my lord, the
intrusion of a subject which is painful to us all. With some
money, and a few provisions, I left my father's cottage; and
since that time have wandered over the country a forlorn and
miserable being, passing my nights in the huts which chance
threw in my way, and designing to travel onward, and to enlist
myself in the service of my country. Night overtook me on these
wastes, and as I walked on comfortless and bewildered, I was
alarmed by distant cries of distress. I quickened my pace; but
the sound which should have directed my steps was ceased, and
chilling silence ensued. As I stood musing, and uncertain which
course to take, I observed a feeble light break through the gloom;
I endeavoured to follow its rays; it led me to these ruins, whose
solemn appearance struck me with a momentary dread. A confused murmur of voices from within struck my ear; as I stood
hesitating whether to enter, I again heard those shrieks which
had alarmed me. I followed the sound; it led me to the entrance
of this cloister, at the extremity of which I discovered a party of
men engaged in fight; I drew my sword and rushed forward; and
the sensations which I felt, on perceiving the lady Mary, cannot
be expressed!' 'Still—still Heaven destines you the deliverer of
Mary!' said the Earl, gratitude swelling in his eyes; 'O! that I
could remove that obstacle which withholds you from your just
reward!' A responsive sigh stole from Alleyn, and he remained
silent. Never was the struggle of opposing feelings more violent,
than that which now agitated the bosom of the Earl. The worth
of Alleyn arose more conspicuously bright from every shade
with which misfortune had veiled it. His noble and disinterested
enthusiasm in the cause of justice, had attached him to the Earl,
and had engaged him in a course of enterprizes and of dangers,
which it required valour to undertake, and skill and persever-
ance to perform; and which had produced services for which no
adequate reward could be found. He had rescued the Earl from
captivity and death; and had twice preserved Mary in dangers.
All these circumstances arose in strong reflection to the mind of

Osbert; but the darkness of prejudice and ancient pride, opposed their influence, and weakened their effect.

The joy which Mary felt on seeing Alleyn in safety, and still worthy of the esteem she had ever bore him, was dashed by the bitterness of reflection; and reflection imparted a melancholy which added to the langour of illness. At the dawn of day they quitted the abbey, and set forward on their return to the castle; the Earl insisting upon Alleyn's accompanying them. On the way, the minds of the party were variously and silently engaged. The Earl ruminated on the conduct of Alleyn, and the late scene. Mary dwelt chiefly on the virtues of her lover, and on the dangers she had escaped; and Alleyn mused on his defeated purposes, and anticipated future trials. The Earl's thoughts, however, were not so wholly occupied, as to prevent his questioning the servant who had been employed by the Count, concerning the further particulars of his scheme. The words of the Count, importing that he had once already endangered his life, had not escaped the notice of the Earl; though they were uttered in a moment of too much distraction to suffer him to demand an explanation. He now enquired of the man, concerning the mysterious scene of the vaults. 'You, I suppose, are not ignorant who were the persons from whom I received my wound.' 'I, my lord, had no concern in that affair; wicked as I am, I could not raise my hands against your life.' 'But you know who did.' 'I—I—ye—yes, my lord, I was afterwards told. But they did not mean to hurt your lordship.' 'Not mean to hurt me!—What then were their designs, and who were the people?' 'That accident happened long before the Count ever spoke to me of his purpose. Indeed, my lord, I had no hand in it; and Heaven knows how I grieved for your lordship; and—' 'Well—well, inform me, who were the persons in the vaults, and what were their design.' 'I was told by a fellow servant; but he made me promise to be secret; but it is proper your lordship should know all; and I hope your lordship will forgive me for having listened to it,—"Robert," said he, as we were talking one day of what had happened,—"Robert," said he, "there is more in this matter than you, or any body thinks; but it is not for me to tell all I know." With that, I begged he would tell me what he knew; he still kept refusing. I promised him faithfully I would not tell; and so at last he told me—"Why, there is my lord Count there, he is in love with our young lady; and to be sure as sweet a lady she is, as ever eyes looked upon; but she don't like him; and so finding himself refused, he is determined to marry her at any rate; and means some night to get into the castle, and carry her off." ' 'What, then!—was it the Count who wounded me?—Be quick in your relation.' 'No, my lord, it was not the Count himself—but two of his people, whom he had sent to examine the castle; and particularly the windows of my young lady's apartment, from whence he designed to have carried her, when every thing was ready for execution. Those men were let within the walls through a way under ground, which leads into the vaults, by my fellow servant, as I afterwards was told; and they escaped through the same way. Their meeting with your lordship was accidental, and they fought only in self-defence; for they had no orders to attack any body.' 'And who is the villain that connived at this scheme!' 'It was my fellow servant, who fled with the Count's people, whom he himself let within the ramparts. Forgive me, my lord; but I did not dare tell; he threatened my life, if I betrayed the secret.'

After a journey of fatigue and unpleasant reflections, they arrived, on the second morning at the castle of Athlin. The Countess, during the absence of her son, had endured a state of dreadful suspense. The Baroness, in her friendship, had endeavoured to soothe her distress, by her constant presence; she was engaged in this amiable office when the trampling of horses in the court reached the ears of Matilda. 'It is my son,' said she, rising from her chair!—'it is my son; he brings me life or death!' She said no more, but rushed into the hall, and in a moment after clasped her almost expiring daughter to her bosom. The transport of the scene repelled utterance; sobs and tears were all that could be given. The general joy, however, was suddenly interrupted by the Baroness, who had followed Matilda into the hall; and who now fell senseless to the ground; delight yielded to surprize, and to the business of assisting the object of it. On recovering, the Baroness looked wildly round her;—'Was it a vision that I saw, or a reality?' The whole company moved their eyes round the hall, but could discover nothing extraordinary. 'It was himself; his very air, his features; that benign countenance which I have so often contemplated in imagination!' Her eyes still seemed in search of some ideal object; and they began to doubt whether a sudden phrenzy had not seized her brain. 'Ah! again!' said she, and instantly relapsed. Their eyes were now turned towards the door, on which she had gazed; it was Alleyn who entered, with water which he had brought for the Countess, and on whom the attention of all present was centered. He approached ignorant of what had happened; and his surprize was great, when the Baroness, reviving, fixed her eyes mournfully upon him, and asked him to uncover his arm.—'It is,—it is my Philip!' said she, with strong emotion; 'I have, indeed, found my long lost child; that strawberry on his arm confirms the decision. Send for the man who calls himself your father, and for my servant Patrick.' The sensations of the mother and the son may be more easily conceived than described; those of Mary were little inferior to theirs; and the whole company awaited with trembling eagerness the arrival of the two persons whose testimony was to decide this interesting affair. They came. 'This young man you call your son?' said the Baroness. 'I do, an' please your ladyship,' he replied, with a degree of confusion which belied his words. When Patrick came, his instant surprize on seeing the old man, declared the truth. 'Do you know this person?' said the Baroness to Patrick. 'Yes, my lady, I know him too well; it was to him I gave your infant son.' The old man started with surprize—'Is that youth the son of your ladyship?' 'Yes!' 'Then God forgive me for having thus long detained him from you! but I was ignorant of his birth, and received him into my cottage as a foundling succoured by lord Malcolm's compassion.' The whole company crowded round them. Alleyn fell at the feet of his mother, and bathed her hand with his tears.— 'Gracious God; for what hast thou reserved me!' He could say no more. The Baroness raised him, and again pressed him in transport to her heart. It was some time before either of them could speak; and all present were too much affected to interrupt the silence. At length, the Baroness presented Laura to her brother. 'Such a mother! and have I such a sister!' said he. Laura wept silently upon his neck the joy of her heart. The Earl was the first who recovered composure sufficient to congratulate Alleyn; and embracing him—'O happy moment, when I can indeed embrace you as my brother!' The whole company now poured forth their joy and their congratulations;—all but Mary, whose emotions almost overcame her, and were too powerful for utterance.

The company now adjourned to the drawing-room; and Mary withdrew to take that repose she so much required. She was sufficiently recovered in a few hours to join her friends in the banquetting-room.

After the transports of the scene were subsided—'I have yet much to hope, and much to fear,' said Philip Malcolm, who was yet Alleyn in every thing but in name, 'You madam,' addressing the Baroness,—'you will willingly become my advocate with her whom I have so long and so ardently loved.' 'May I hope,' continued he, taking tenderly the hand of Mary, who stood trembling by,—'that you have not been insensible to my long attachment, and that you will confirm the happiness which is now offered me?' A smile of ineffable sweetness broke through the melancholy which had long clouded her features, and which even the present discovery had not been able entirely to dissipate, and her eye gave the consent which her tongue refused to utter.

The conversation, for the remainder of the day, was occupied by the subject of the discovery, and with a recital of Mary's adventure. It was determined that on the morrow the marriage of the Earl should be concluded.

On this happy discovery, the Earl ordered the gates of the castle to be thrown open; mirth and festivity resounded through the walls, and the evening closed in universal rejoicings.

On the following morn, the chapel of the castle was decorated for the marriage of the Earl; who with Laura, came attended by Philip, now Baron Malcolm, by Mary, and the whole family. When they approached the altar, the Earl, addressing himself to his bride,—'Now, my Laura,' said he, 'we may celebrate those nuptials which have twice been so painfully interrupted, and which are to crown me with felicity. This day shall unite our families in a double marriage, and reward the worth of my friend. It is now seen, that those virtues which stimulated him to prosecute for another the cause of justice mysteriously urged him to the recovery of his rights. Virtue may for a time be pursued by misfortune,—and justice be obscured by the transient triumphs of vice,—but the power whose peculiar attributes they are, clears away the clouds of error, and even in this world reveals his THRONE OF JUSTICE.

The Earl stepped forward, and joining the hands of Philip and Mary,—'Surely,' said he, 'this is a moment of perfect happiness!—I can now reward those virtues which I have ever loved; and those services to which every gift must be inadequate, but this I now bestow.'

FINIS

EXPLANATORY NOTES

1 *epigraph*: from 'Abelard to Eloisa' in James Cawthorn's *Poems* (1771), 59.

3 *romantic*: this word has the meaning of 'wild and imaginative' at this period. So the *Critical Review* praised *The Castles of Athlin and Dunbayne* for 'some fancy and much romantic imagery'.

sea: many of the Scottish castles observed by eighteenth-century travellers enjoyed this setting, for example Slanes as viewed by Samuel Johnson: 'built upon the margin of the sea, so that the walls of one of the towers seem only a continuation of a perpendicular rock, the foot of which is beaten by the waves', *A Journey to the Western Islands of Scotland* (1775), 14.

Earl of Athlin: the virtuous Athlin is a peer, one of an order of thirteen earls of Scotland, in contrast to Malcolm, whose title of baron was used by anyone who held a fief with a court in which public justice was dispensed. So Athlin represents the order of emerging statehood, but Malcolm the local despotism of the clan system.

feudal greatness: this sets the narrative in the middle ages, uniquely in Radcliffe's published fiction.

clans: Scottish tribal groupings claiming a common ancestor. Their internecine warfare was notorious.

chiefs: 'Every clan consisted of several tribes; and the head of each tribe was the representative of a family descended from that of the chief. His patronymic (which marked his descent) denominated the tribe of which he was a chieftain, and his lands . . . were let to his friends and relatives in the same manner that the lands of the chief were let to his friends'. John Home, *History of the Rebellion* (1745), 392.

finesse: artful stratagem.

slew him: Thomas Pennant recounts a similar onslaught on the Colquhouns as late as 1594 by the clan of the Macgregors: 'the laird of Colquhoun escaped and retired to a strong castle; but being closely pursued by a party of the enemy, they broke into the castle and found him in a vault, where they instantly put him to death with many circumstances of cruelty'. *A Tour in Scotland 1769* (1772), i. 366.

4 *genius*: mental power.

benevolence: the key virtue of the eighteenth-century cult of sensibility.

5 *risque:* risk.

favourite art: as a medieval nobleman, Athlin may be held to enjoy the poetry of Ossian, which appeared as *Fragments of Ancient Poetry* in 1760, edited—and forged—by James Macpherson. As a cultivated man of the eighteenth century Osbert owes his appreciation of mountain—and especially Highland—landscape to Thomas Gray's celebrated Scottish letter of 1765, Ossian, Beattie's *The Minstrel* (1771–7), and William Collins's unfinished 'Ode on the Popular Superstitions of the Highlanders considered as a Subject for Poetry' (1788). John Home's blank verse drama, *Douglas*, of 1756 was also very influential and in frequent production to the end of the century.

fancy: imagination.

6 *repulse of fear*: this whole section bears a close resemblance to Johnson's passage in *A Journey to the Western Islands of Scotland*:

> I sat down on a bank, such as a writer of Romance might have delighted to feign . . . The day was calm, the air soft, and all was rudeness, silence and solitude. Before me, and on either side, were high hills, which by hindering the eye from ranging, forced the mind to find entertainment for itself . . . We were in this place at ease, and by choice and had no evils to suffer and fear; yet the imaginations excited by the view of an unknown and untravelled wilderness are not such as arise in the artificial solitude of parks and gardens, a flattering notion of self-sufficiency, a placid indulgence of voluntary delusions, a secure expansion of the fancy, or a cool concentration of the mental powers. The phantoms which haunt a desert are want, and misery, and danger; the evils of dereliction rush upon the thoughts; man is made unwillingly acquainted with his won weakness, and meditation shows him only how little he can perform.   (87–8)

cottages: 'a hut is constructed with loose stones, ranged for the most part with some tendency to circularity. It must be placed where the wind cannot act upon it with violence, because it has no cement; and where water will run easily away, because it has no floor but the naked ground'. *Journey to the Western Islands*, 66.

Elysian vale: the delightful pastoral landscape inhabited by the virtuous dead in classical mythology.

7 *partook*: partaken.

  force of arms: an anachronistic view of the clan system but typical of Radcliffe's moderate radicalism.

  Fitz-Henrys . . . friends to virtue: despite its Norman sound, this is a plausible name for a Scottish clan. There was a Fitz Allan among barons listed as called to the Siege of Caerlaveroc in the reign of Edward I. (See Pennant, *Tour in Scotland*, ii. 411.)

9 *chivalry*: the system of knighthood and its duties.

10 *the habit of a Highland lass*: 'the single women wear only a ribband round their head, which they call a snood. The *tonnag*, or plaid, hung over their shoulders, and is fastened before with a brotche; but in bad weather is drawn over their heads'. Pennant, *Tour in Scotland*, i. 192.

  Graces: Aglaia, Thalia, and Euphrosyne, the daughters of Venus, who preside over acts of benevolence in classical mythology.

11 *figure of his dying father . . . stamped his purpose irrevocably*: Radcliffe seems to be indebted to *Hamlet*, with the ghastly apparition of the King reduced to an inner mental image.

12 *the clan assembled in arms*: Radcliffe later mentions a bell as calling the clan to the *cam a whin* or rendezvous. Pennant describes a burnt and bloody pole as carried from man to man signalling the shame and penalty of non-attendance. Radcliffe, as usual, is anxious to stress virtue rather than fear as a motive force.

13 *dangerous rock*: the usual situation for a Scottish castle, as travellers agree.

17 *mattrass*: mattress.

  the sufferings of suspense . . . means of endurance: the Baron's scheme is mirrored by that of the author's narrative. Radcliffe's chief tool for the evocation of fear in the reader is suspense: there is little actual violence in her novels.

18 *short dagger*: 'the *mattucashlash* or armpit dagger, was worn there ready to be used on coming to close quarters'. Pennant, *Tour in Scotland*, ii. 191.

  lute: a stringed instrument in vogue from the fourteenth century, often used to accompany the voice.

20 *palfry*: more often 'palfrey', a light saddle-horse for ladies.

  tenderness: the fortunate outcome of this abduction is signalled by the setting of the episode at twilight, the key time of day for Radcliffe's poetics.

25 *subterraneous way . . . some distance*: 'in the woods adjacent to this seat [Newbottle] are some subterraneous apartments and passages cut out of the live rock: they seem to have been excavated by the ancient inhabitants of the country either as receptacles for their provisions, or a retreat for themselves and families in time of war'. Pennant, *Tour in Scotland*, i. 62.

28 *fosse*: ditch.

31 *monitor*: the heart as instructor and advisor.

33 *when first the vernal morn of life*: the style of the three poems in the novel is eighteenth century rather than authentically medieval. Here the mode is close to the hymns of Isaac Watts or especially the melancholy William Cowper, with the short-lined quatrains and abrupt change in mood in the last stanza.

35 *the champion of virtue*: the original title of Clara Reeve's novel, *The Old English Baron* (1775), although in Reeve the champion is the Alleyn figure, the seemingly low-born Edmund Twyford.

39 *admiration*: wonder as much as appreciation.

   sonnet: not necessarily a poem of fourteen lines.

41 *stanchion*: the upright iron bar between the mullions of a window.

   parley: a meeting with enemies to talk.

42 *he dies*: a dilemma reminiscent of the amatory bargain Angelo seeks to make with Isabella for the release of her brother in Shakespeare's *Measure for Measure*.

46 *they fell like the drops of Heaven . . . dying foliage*: perhaps a reference to Portia's speech, concerning a similar impossible choice in *The merchant of Venice*: 'The quality of mercy is not strained. / It droppeth as the gentle rain from heaven / Upon the place beneath. 'IV. i. Tears in the sensibility tradition are inherently beneficent and lead to human sympathy and compassion.

   sofa: an anachronism.

   chears: cheers.

49 *centrical*: central.

51 *pannel*: panel.

56 *rights of nature*: this is the language of Jean-Jacques Rousseau's *Social Contract* (1762). However, Radcliffe does not totally deprecate the feudal system; rather, hers is the attitude of enlightened paternalism common to Johnson, who criticized the forced clearance

of the Highlands, and Pennant, who writes approvingly of an ideal landlord, Mr Macleod:

> He feels for the distresses of his people, and insensible of his own, with uncommon disinterestedness has relieved his tenants from their oppressive rents. . . . The Highlanders may bless the hand that loosened their bonds: for tyranny more often than protection was the attendance of their vassalage. *Tour in Scotland*, ii. 294.

It is doubtful whether the Scots would have agreed that their repression by the British after the 1745 rebellion was a liberation.

60 *Switzerland . . . distinguished his ancestors*: as a protestant state, Switzerland appeared a centre of virtue to eighteenth-century opinion, especially associated with Rousseau and his Savoyard vicar in *Émile*. Its mountainous terrain would feature prominently in Radcliffe's *Romance of the Forest* (1791).

61 *encreased*: increased.

64 *efficient*: effective.

72 *traditionary visions of his nation*: 'the *Second Sight* is an impression made either by the mind upon the eye, or the eye upon the mind, by which things distant or future are perceived, and seen as if they were present'. Johnson, *Journey to the Western Islands*, 248.

73 *dubious*: doubtful.

74 *single combat*: a chivalric mode of fighting, not uncommon in clan warfare. See William Gilpin, *Observations on the Highlands of Scotland* (1789), 189 ff.

76 *windows . . . looked upon the sea*: See Johnson's account of Slanes Castle: 'From the windows the eye wanders over the sea that separates Scotland from Norway, and when the winds beat with violence must enjoy all the terrifick grandeur of the tempestuous ocean'. *Journey to the Western Islands*, 36.

enthusiastic awe: in the tradition of James Thomson's poem, *The Seasons*, and the graveyard poets such as Blair, Young, and Gray, the power of natural forces makes the human mind aware of its weakness and physical limitation, and turns the mind to an awareness of the Divine. 'To our imagination,' writes Edmund Burke, 'his power is by far the most striking' of God's attributes, and is the source of all sublime effects. See *A Philosophical Enquiry into the Origin of our Ideas of the Sublime and Beautiful* (1757), 62. The sea has the qualities of vastness, sound, seeming infinity, and danger, which evoke the sublime.

85 *clan of the Baron*: recognized by their plaid which consists of 'twelve or thirteen yards of a narrow stuff, wrapt around the middle, and reaches to the knees ... the colour of their dress was various, as the word *breaccan* implies, being dyed with stripes of the most vivid hues'. Pennant, *Tour in Scotland*, i. 189. The colours differed from clan to clan but were mostly not the tartans known today, nor was the plaid like the pleated kilt, which was an eighteenth-century invention.

86 *arrow from his bow*: this mode of warfare continued in Scotland until the 1650s.

90 *the features of vice*: Malcolm's end is that of the man of vice in Lord Shaftesbury's *Characteristics of Men; Manners, Opinions, Times, etc.* (1711) and the later William Gilpin's *Moral Contrasts* (1798).

91 *sublunary*: under the moon, and thus earthly.

93 *Morning*: other such songs of the period are more rustic or satirical in character, although Thomas Gray's 'incense-breathing morn' is close; and Gray's is the poetic model for the song, especially his 'Ode on the Pleasure Arising from Vicissitude'.

Aurora: the Roman goddess of Dawn who rode in a rose-coloured chariot to awake the world before the sun's rising and to pour the dew.

blithsome: pleasant.

Bards: A Scottish touch, as although Bard is a general term for an ancient poet much used by eighteenth-century poetry, the Scottish chiefs used to employ bards to record their family history in song.

97 *relume*: relight.

102 *ruins of an abbey ... evening*: this is the first appearance of a key Gothic site in Radcliffe's later fiction, as well as the favourite haunt of the melancholic: 'Beneath yon ruin'd abbey's moss-grown piles/Oft let me sit, at twilight hour of eve', Thomas Warton, 'The Pleasures of Melancholy' (1747).

THE WORLD'S CLASSICS

A Select List

HANS ANDERSEN: Fairy Tales
Translated by L. W. Kingsland
Introduction by Naomi Lewis
Illustrated by Vilhelm Pedersen and Lorenz Frølich

ARTHUR J. ARBERRY (Transl.): The Koran

LUDOVICO ARIOSTO: Orlando Furioso
Translated by Guido Waldman

ARISTOTLE: The Nicomachean Ethics
Translated by David Ross

JANE AUSTEN: Emma
Edited by James Kinsley and David Lodge

Mansfield Park
Edited by James Kinsley and John Lucas

Northanger Abbey, Lady Susan, The Watsons,
and **Sanditon**
Edited by John Davie

HONORÉ DE BALZAC: Père Goriot
Translated and Edited by A. J. Krailsheimer

CHARLES BAUDELAIRE: The Flowers of Evil
Translated by James McGowan
Introduction by Jonathan Culler

WILLIAM BECKFORD: Vathek
Edited by Roger Lonsdale

R. D. BLACKMORE: Lorna Doone
Edited by Sally Shuttleworth

KEITH BOSLEY (Transl.): The Kalevala

JAMES BOSWELL: Life of Johnson
The Hill/Powell edition, revised by David Fleeman
Introduction by Pat Rogers

MARY ELIZABETH BRADDON: Lady Audley's Secret
Edited by David Skilton

ANNE BRONTË: The Tenant of Wildfell Hall
Edited by Herbert Rosengarten and Margaret Smith

CHARLOTTE BRONTË: Jane Eyre
Edited by Margaret Smith

Shirley
Edited by Margaret Smith and Herbert Rosengarten

EMILY BRONTË: Wuthering Heights
Edited by Ian Jack

GEORG BÜCHNER:
Danton's Death, Leonce and Lena, Woyzeck
Translated by Victor Price

JOHN BUNYAN: The Pilgrim's Progress
Edited by N. H. Keeble

EDMUND BURKE: A Philosophical Enquiry into the
Origin of our Ideas of the Sublime and Beautiful
Edited by Adam Phillips

FANNY BURNEY: Camilla
Edited by Edward A. Bloom and Lilian D. Bloom

THOMAS CARLYLE: The French Revolution
Edited by K. J. Fielding and David Sorensen

LEWIS CARROLL: Alice's Adventures in Wonderland
and Through the Looking Glass
Edited by Roger Lancelyn Green
Illustrated by John Tenniel

HORACE WALPOLE : The Castle of Otranto
Edited by W. S. Lewis

IZAAK WALTON and CHARLES COTTON:
The Compleat Angler
Edited by John Buxton
Introduction by John Buchan

OSCAR WILDE: Complete Shorter Fiction
Edited by Isobel Murray

The Picture of Dorian Gray
Edited by Isobel Murray

MARY WOLLSTONECRAFT:
Mary *and* The Wrongs of Woman
Edited by Gary Kelly

VIRGINIA WOOLF: Mrs Dalloway
Edited by Claire Tomalin

Orlando
Edited by Rachel Bowlby

ÉMILE ZOLA:
The Attack on the Mill and Other Stories
Translated by Douglas Parmée

Nana
Translated and Edited by Douglas Parmée